THE WORMLING I:

The Book of the King

THE WORMLING
BOOK I

The Book of the King

JERRY B. JENKINS
CHRIS FABRY

Tyndale House Publishers, Inc.
Carol Stream, Illinois

Visit Tyndale's website for kids at www.tyndale.com/kids.

The Wormling I: The Book of the King

Designed by Ron Kaufmann

Edited by Lorie Popp

Published in association with the literary agency of Alive Communications, Inc., 7680 Goddard Street, Suite 200, Colorado Springs, CO 80920.

The Wormling I: The Book of the King is a work of fiction. Where real people, events, establishments, organizations, or locales appear, they are used fictitiously. All other elements of the novel are drawn from the author's imagination.

For manufacturing information regarding this product, please call 1-800-323-9400.

Library of Congress Cataloging-in-Publication Data

Jenkins, Jerry B.
   The Wormling I : the book of the king / Jerry B. Jenkins ; Chris Fabry.
      p. cm.
   Summary: Guided by a mysterious book and invisible guardians, meek high-schooler Owen Reeder learns that there is another world besides his ordinary one, where he is destined to face an evil dragon in order to make his own world safe and whole again.
   ISBN 978-1-4143-0155-6 (softcover : alk. paper)
   [1. Adventure and adventurers—Fiction. 2. Books and reading—Fiction. 3. Conduct of life—Fiction. 4. Good and evil—Fiction. 5. Dragons—Fiction.]
I. Fabry, Chris, date. II. Title. III. Title: Wormling one. IV. Title: Book of the king.
PZ7.J4138Wor 2007
[Fic]—dc22   2006024475

Printed in the United States of America

17   16   15   14
11   10   9   8   7

"We are not human beings having a spiritual experience.
We are spiritual beings having a human experience."

PIERRE TEILHARD DE CHARDIN

✦

"Life is pain, Highness. Anyone who says
differently is selling something."

WESTLEY IN *The Princess Bride*

1

The Beginning

To tell the story of Owen Reeder—
the whole story and not just the
parts that tickle the mind and make
you laugh from the belly like one who
has had too much to drink—we have
to go into much unpleasantness.

So if you are faint of heart and can't
stand bloody battles and cloaked figures
in the darkness and invisible creatures
(or visible ones who don't have much
of a sense of humor), and if you don't
like to cry over a story when someone
you love is taken, then perhaps our tale
is not for you. But if you'd like to read
about a young man with seemingly no
future but dreams he can barely hold
in his head and about a war between

opponents as far apart as east is from west—one side that loves evil and seeks to kill and destroy the hearts of good people and another that wants desperately to free those good people from tyranny and injustice—and about the deepest love the heart can imagine, then we welcome you.

Since this story concerns a young man named Owen and it occurs today in our time, you might think we would begin on some basketball court or in some school hallway, and I suppose we could have begun there, for Owen certainly found himself on many courts and in many hallways.

But we begin in a world far away, in a castle lit by candles, in darkened stone hallways that echo sadly with memories of a baby's cry and a mother's tender kiss. A man stands on a parapet, which is not two pets but a low stone wall on a balcony meant to keep those foolish enough to stand out there from falling to their deaths. The man is regal, which is to say he has good posture and wears embroidered robes and a crown, so anyone with half a brain can guess who he is. He looks out at his kingdom shrouded in darkness and shudders. Perhaps it is the chill wind coming across the water or the moonless night. Or perhaps he has a cold.

But as the man turns and walks into the inner chamber, there seems to be more wrong than the weather or his health. He silently slips into the hall, alerting guards standing at attention on either side.

"Anything wrong, sire?" one whispers.

"No, I simply have a request." The man speaks quietly, not wishing to wake his wife or any of the nobles in the castle. He imagines their making the discovery in the morning, but for now he focuses on the task and gives simple instructions.

When he is finished, the man steps back inside the chamber and gazes at his sleeping wife. His face contorts, and it appears his heart will burst from some long-held emotion. He leans over the canopied bed and gently kisses the woman. She has an anxious look, even in sleep. The man slips something she will read in the morning under her pillow.

If you were to inch closer in the flickering candlelight, you would see a tear escape the man and fall silently to the bed. The man's gaze sweeps the room, as if this is the last time he will see it, as if he is saying good-bye to the lampstands and the velvet curtains and the map of a huge kingdom mounted in a massive wooden frame.

He walks to a baby's crib in the corner and runs a hand along its dusty coverlet. The man appears to have lost something valuable, to have spent years searching every nook and cranny of his kingdom. He seems to be longing for something from his past.

But what?

If your eyes were to linger on that crib, on the fine wood inlaid with exquisite detail, you would miss the man's instant exit, not through the main door past the two guards but through another passageway, secret and cloaked from view.

The man pads down narrow stone stairs, feeling his way in the dark, reaching for support from the cool walls on either side. You might be scared that a rat would scurry past, but the man walks resolutely, hurrying.

We will not tell you how many levels he descends, but when the air changes to a musty dankness and he feels water on the walls and mud under his feet, his gait slows and he reaches a chamber that looks and feels rarely visited.

He pulls around him a dark curtain fastened to the wall, hiding himself from view. We see no other living being, and the room is totally, blindingly dark, yet it appears the man is hiding. Let us be clear. He is in the bowels of the castle, behind a thick curtain, in total darkness. We hear scurrying and the flap of heavy clothing falling to the earthen floor. Then grunting and something heavy being pulled or pushed from its rightful place and the fluttering of the curtain as a soft breeze enters.

One more sound—a click and the opening of some compartment. Something is removed and placed heavily on a stone, and fabric is tied. We hear more struggling—as if someone is trying to squeeze through a small space—then stone upon stone again.

Inside is still, save for a trickle of water down the wall and the soft whirring of insects inside the stone cracks. But if you were to put your ear to one of those cracks, or if you, like an insect, were to crawl between the stones and reach the chill of the night air, you would hear the soft lapping of water against a shore and the even softer sound of oars rowing away in the darkness.

This man, now in tattered clothes with a heavy blanket over his shoulders, does not look as if he deserves to live in a castle. When he reaches the shore on the other side—and it has been no small feat to row to this distance against the wind—he steers into a small inlet and covers the boat with branches and dead limbs that appear to have been gathered in anticipation of this very trip. The man slings a wrapped pouch over his back and quickly walks away, the food stuffed in his pockets telling us he does not plan to be back for breakfast.

You may ask, if this is such a cloudy, moonless night, how is the man able to navigate the soaked earth and craggy rocks without falling off the sheer cliffs only yards to his left? Has he walked this route in his mind, planning it from the parapet of the castle?

By the time the sun casts crimson shadows, he is at the wood and into the thick trees. A fox scurries to its den with a twitching rabbit hanging from its mouth.

When the sun peeks over the horizon, the man is deep in shadows, adjusting his pack as he glides through white-barked trees as thick as clover. He reaches an ivy-covered wall on the other side of the grove, out of place in the wood. He scans the mountain, taking in its majesty, then reaches to move the ivy to reveal a circular crest bearing the image of a beast, a dragon. To some this would appear to be an entrance, but it is not. It is a barrier, a rock so thick that the man could work a lifetime and not move or dislodge it.

The man places his pack on the ground, unties it, and pulls out a book, the edges of its pages golden, the thick leather cover creaking as he opens it. He runs a hand over a page and the letters carefully inscribed there.

He turns as if he has heard something behind him, then pulls the blanket closer to his face and turns back to the book. As he begins to speak, the words come to life and something magical—and wonderful—happens.

2

The Dragon

We will turn to Owen shortly, for his story is the reason we are writing, but the image on the rock brings another scene we must visit—the actual dragon the image represents. The image comes to life in the Dragon's invisible realm high above. We call it invisible, but it is so only for humans and only when those who live above stay above. You should be happy you cannot see this kingdom, which invades your own and is all around you.

As you moved closer to this beast— if you could stand the stench—you would see pure evil. It is not easy to describe such a vile, despicable being to adults or children, but it is necessary in order to see the truth about him and understand what Owen is up against.

Imagine a creature so horrible, so terrifying and hideous that he makes *repugnant* sound like a compliment. Sulfurous breath—which means he exhales something akin to burned charcoal and smoke from a thousand campfires gone bad. And that's on a good day. Huge nostrils flare with each breath, and a drool of yellow saliva—yes, yellow—slithers down a crusted chin. Red, glowing reptilian eyes are shrouded with scaly lids, and a great tail stretches from the massive, undulating body. The monstrous head looks like a cross between a horse's and a human's. And the wings—veined, cracked, and enormous, though he has them tucked away when he's resting—are able to propel him with frightening speed.

We would not be telling you this if it weren't absolutely necessary. But you must come closer to this being, because he is central to the conflict. If this upsets you, perhaps you prefer stories about furry animals running about, speaking funny lines, and playing games. We have only just begun. By the end there will be blood and an attack so vicious that your first reaction will be to turn away from these pages. But we promise—you will like Owen. You will love him from the moment you meet him. His heart is so genuine. He is such a good lad that you would want him as your friend, even if you had scores of them. And so we continue.

Suffice it to say that this being, the image on the rock come to life, whom we will refer to from now on as the Dragon, does not like to be stirred in the night. You could say he likes his beauty sleep, but there is no beauty about him. Perhaps he needs his ugly sleep.

Into the Dragon's lair comes RHM—no, not his right-hand man. This RHM is Reginald Handler Mephistopheles. Think of him as the younger brother to the Dragon, just as ugly but with more human qualities—a beaklike nose, brows that look like a forest of unruly trees, and gnarly, elongated fingernails that resemble the claws of some wild bird. Oh, and a heart so rancid and devoted to his new master that nothing—absolutely nothing—could soften it.

RHM tiptoes into this sleeping chamber, so cold he can see his breath. He stumbles over a weather-beaten rug (which has bits of rotten flesh and the bones of RHM's predecessor embedded in it) and tries to regain his balance by grabbing a nightstand sporting a crystal vase. Why the Dragon owns a crystal vase we shall have to leave for another time, because at the sound of the crash the old beast awakens, snorting and sniffing and rearing back as if ready to shoot fire.

"I'm sorry, Your Majesty!" RHM says. "Please forgive me."

"Why do you wake me?" The Dragon's voice booms through the cavernous room like a cannon, a metallic rasp to it as if his vocal chords have been scraped raw.

"There is movement in the King's castle, sire," RHM says, head down. "Our Stalker said—"

The Dragon sits up, eyes ablaze and snout now inches from his newly appointed helper's face. Even the loyal subjects of a tyrant have trouble hiding their trembling fear, for they never know when they will become the enemy. "Yes?" the Dragon explodes. "The Stalker said what?"

"The King is gone. He slipped into some secret passage, I suppose, and—"

"You suppose?"

"The King gave an order to his soldiers and the Stalker followed them, but when he returned . . ."

The Dragon's gaze darts, red veins bulging, making the thin, black slit at the center of each eye even more menacing. The old beast makes calculations, sifting through the data in his mind until an impish grin creeps across his face. "It has begun. The King has exhausted his men searching for the boy. He himself has spent more time away from the castle than in it the last few years. He's finally given in to the truth."

RHM rubs greasy hands together. "Which makes him vulnerable, sire."

The Dragon looks out on a thousand glowing fires, encampments of his sleeping troops. They are always ready for battle or engaged in one. He raises a corner of his lip, showing a tooth so sharp it makes ice picks envious. "This has been my plan all along. Summon the Stalkers. Send them to the four portals and have them report to me immediately."

"With gladness, sire."

"Wait!" the Dragon says. "Send one to the castle. Have him look for this book the King has fancied so long."

The Dragon stands, putting his considerable weight on legs like boulders. He turns to the window overlooking the King's domain and sucks in a breath. "We have waited for this day. The King has made a terrible error, and I will see him in his grave."

"The Son too?" RHM says.

The Dragon's crusty, coughing laugh would have made you ill. When the rattle stops, the Dragon sneers, "The King has been protected here. When he dies and his Son after him, this realm becomes mine. Three worlds will unite under my rule." He sweeps an arm toward the window, bidding his aide to look, and the flutter of a webbed wing sends a puff of air toward RHM that would have turned you away, gasping. But the malodorous smell is like perfume to the aide, and he gazes out the window with rapturous delight.

"I have waited for this," the Dragon says. "All our striving will be worth it when I see the last dying breath of the King. And then they will see what it means to have a ruler. A true king."

3

The Arm in the Night

If you were sitting in the small, crowded Briarwood Café on the night our story begins, you might gravitate to where three tables have been pushed together to accommodate high school students having just completed their next-to-last night of the fall musical. Several girls wear long, flowing gowns. The young men wear tennis shoes and sweatpants—they are stagehands and not committed thespians. Their presence at the rehearsals and the play is, in actuality, so they can work with the young females, so you can understand why they are at the restaurant this evening. They are boisterous, excited.

A few families dine amid the din. Some patrons scowl at the noise, but most endure it with good-natured looks.

The stools at the front, the kind you see in old-fashioned diners, are full of weary travelers. Some grimace each time the door opens and a blast of cold air attacks, but the general mood of the place is pleasant.

The boys—the ones in sweatpants and with bad manners—notice the waitress, another classmate, as she scurries back and forth to the kitchen. She's wearing a dark uniform with an apron tied at the front.

"She has the best eyes," one boy says loud enough so she can hear.

"You're looking at her eyes?" another says, and the group erupts in laughter.

But the first boy is right. Her eyes are the color of the ocean, blue-green pools lost in the inlet of her long dark hair, pulled into a bun. A few strands have come loose and hang across her face. Her eyebrows are dark and finely shaped, and her lips are naturally red, without the aid of lipstick. Her cheeks are plump and full of color, remnants of her childhood, for the rest of her has grown into a young woman. Her name tag says *Clara*, which doesn't seem to fit. (We don't mean to offend you if you happen to be a Clara. The name just doesn't seem right for this girl.) Her last name was Secrest. Clara Secrest.

As the boys continue to whisper among themselves about Clara's looks, the girls appear to try to draw attention back to themselves.

Look carefully now, as we are the only ones who notice the slight boy entering the café, quickly pulling the door closed against the wind. A thoughtful lad, wouldn't you agree? He limps, heading for the small carryout counter.

He looks uncomfortable waiting for service, as if he were somehow intruding on the party. He is hardly striking. His hair is light brown and thick, cut just above the ears with the front a little too short, revealing the indelible marks of adolescence on his forehead. He nervously pats his hair, as if he could make it suddenly grow and cover the red bumps. The boy looks younger than those at the tables and pale, as if he spends most of his time inside. His legs are not long, his hands small and soft.

Other than the limp, nothing would make you notice him, except that is precisely what Clara did as she came out of the kitchen. "I'll be with you in a minute," she said, carrying hot food.

The boy straightened as if he suffered from some spine ail-ment. "I'm fine," he said, his voice cracking. "Take your time."

Clara smiled, and it was in that instant that she tumbled to the floor, hamburgers sailing, dishes crashing. It was not clear whose feet she had stumbled over, but one of the boys laughed while the rest of the place fell silent.

If you focused on the girl on the floor and the mess she made, you would miss the reaction of the boy at the counter. His face was like some resolute explorer's, unafraid of uncharted waters. "Are you all right?" he said, helping her up.

Clara nodded, then bent to begin picking up the mess.

"What about my burger?" a long-gowned girl said.

A young man with a big chest and a red face asked for a soda refill and handed Clara the glass.

"I'll clean this up," the boy from the counter said. "Go ahead."

"I can't let you do that."

The boy grabbed a wastebasket from the corner. "Really. Go ahead."

Clara stared at him with those endless ocean eyes and hurried to the kitchen.

"Missed one," the red-faced boy said, shoving a jagged piece of glass with his foot.

Moments later Clara returned with the drink, a broom, and an update on the burger. "We won't charge you," she said to Long Gown.

"I should hope not."

Clara checked out two families at the cash register, retrieved the replacement burger, delivered three checks, and finally reached the carryout counter. "You shouldn't have done that," she said to the boy. "My boss is mad."

The boy was lost in her eyes. "Sorry. Just trying to help."
He looked at the menu again.

Allow us to let you in on a little secret no one else—not
even the boy's father—knew: he had a special reading ability and had already memorized the menu. That gift put him
ahead of everyone else in his class. In fact, many times he
had to hold himself back from answering every question after
reading a text only once.

"You've been here before, haven't you?" Clara said.

"My father lets me get dessert a couple times a month."

Clara leaned on the counter and sighed. She had
worked a full shift, and though she tried to hide it, she
walked as if her feet felt like lead. "You're in my journalism class, right?"

He nodded. "I'm a freshman."

"Sort of young to be in high school, aren't you?"

"I skipped a grade." Actually he could have skipped two or
three grades had his father allowed it.

Clara squinted. "What's your name?"

"Owen. Owen Reeder."

Didn't we tell you that you would love him at first sight?

Clara picked up her green pad. "Well, Owen Reeder,
thanks for helping me out. Now what can I get you?"

Don't you agree that at this point Owen should
have been full of pride and confidence? He may have

been shy and timid, but he had helped a damsel in distress and had even held up his end of the conversation with a pretty girl.

But all that was forgotten when the red-faced, big-armed, barrel-chested boy took his foot off a chair and kicked it away, standing as if ready for a duel. "Reeder? Did you just say you're Owen Reeder?"

Owen spun as if about to be hit by a train.

"You're the kid who writes in the paper," Red Face said.

Owen nodded, but he wanted nothing to do with Red Face. He looked at the menu, then at Clara. "I think I'll have—"

"Know who I am?" Red Face said.

"Sure," Owen said. "Gordan Kalb. I just did an article on your wrestling—"

Gordan moved like a hungry lion. "You made me look like an idiot in that article."

Owen didn't know what the wrestler was talking about, but because he was not only a reader of books but also attuned to danger, Owen knew it was time to leave.

Owen had read that if a person concentrated on one spot on the wall and thought of a beach or some peaceful glen, he could shut out pain and fear. He had tried this at the dentist's office and learned that no amount of focusing lessened the pain of an impacted molar, let alone having Gordan Kalb separate his head from his neck.

"I'd better come back another time," Owen said softly to Clara.

Though Gordan looked twice Owen's size, two others joined him and blocked the front door.

A bell rang in the kitchen, and Clara grabbed Owen's hand and pulled him behind the counter. "Could you help me with something?"

"You can't come in here!" the cook yelled.

"The back door is that way," Clara whispered.

Gordan burst in just as Owen escaped.

When in the course of human events it becomes necessary for a frightened young man to slip the surly bonds of danger and touch the face of freedom, please note that the back door of a restaurant is not always the best exit. It may help one escape three hulking figures at the front door, but it does little else to aid the escapee when the street is blocked by construction equipment.

Owen couldn't go back inside, because Gordan was on his way out.

If you've ever been scared, you understand why Owen felt as if his heart would beat out of his chest. He couldn't breathe. His legs felt tired even before he began running. And his mind raced with what would happen if Gordan or his friends caught him.

Owen tore down a dark alley, dodging trash and whatever

animals scurried among the cans. When Owen finally made it to the street, Gordan was close behind, and the two who had blocked the front door were coming around the corner. Owen turned right and kept running.

Unfortunately, Owen realized he was running the opposite direction from his home, the used-book store his father owned called Tattered Treasures. His father was strict about when Owen could go out (almost never) and when he had to be back (soon). Owen had read enough books about children whose parents were hard-nosed to believe that his father wanted only to protect him from the harshness of the world and the cruelty of his peers (like now).

Owen felt sorry for his father, because Owen's mother had died when he was born, and the man seemed desperately unhappy. Owen tried not to create more trouble for him. Plus, Owen enjoyed the bookstore and the chance to peruse the many shelves.

But all that would end if he was torn to pieces by these boys. To make matters worse, night had fallen heavily. No moon or stars lit the jet-black sky. It was as if someone had turned off the world's light.

"We're gonna get you, Reeder!" Gordan shouted.

If Owen had any inkling how his life was about to change, the things he would soon experience, the foes he would face, the friends he would make, and how even at this point there

were things going on he couldn't see or even imagine, perhaps
he would have seen this run through the streets in a different
light. Instead, his heart raced, his eyes stung, and his gimpy
right foot ached.

In the inky darkness, Owen noticed the smallest glow of a
candle in a second-floor window across the street. He darted
across, ducking low-hanging tree limbs.

"There he goes!" someone yelled.

Owen tripped over the curb but regained his balance and
limped past the building into another alley, this one even
darker.

᭡

As Owen's footsteps echoed off the walls of the alley, Gordan
grabbed his friends by their shirts.

"What are you doing?" one said. "He's getting away!"

Gordan smiled. "We don't have to worry about him
anymore."

"Why? What do you mean?"

Gordan laughed, and they made their way back to the
restaurant.

᭡

Owen could think of only one thing in those terrible moments.
The speech he was to give the next day was forgotten, as was

Clara, the beautiful girl at the restaurant he had noticed his first day of high school. He thought only of escape.

He stumbled over small stones and slid in mud. Strange. A car passed the alley and illuminated the street for an instant.

A tiny modicum of hope sprang within him that he might actually make it home alive, but he kept running, desperate to put as much distance between himself and those three as he could.

There are moments that define a life. A third strike with the bases loaded. An offhand suggestion to go swimming in the quarry. A dare to "jump from there." Such moments, upon reflection, tell us the road of life has taken a turn that will forever change us.

Such was the fate of Owen Reeder, for as he took his last step of what could be called a normal life, something caught him at his waist. A steel beam? A wooden plank? Someone's arm? Whatever it was, he felt like a cartoon character who had just hit a railing. His feet and arms flew forward along with his head; then he snapped back.

Laughter echoed in the distance. A dog barked. But Owen was suspended in midair.

He hung, straining, struggling. That's when he heard the whisper that called every hair on his body to attention.

"Courage, Owen."

At that moment Owen would not have been able to tell

you if this was something he actually heard or the product of his terrified imagination. But something had wished courage on his life, had spoken courage to the marrow of his bones and the center of his soul.

Owen felt he was being shifted by something mechanical back onto mud and bricks again, solid ground. He heard a whoosh, as if something had left him, and for the first time that night the sky shone light—beautiful, illuminating light. Owen couldn't take his eyes from it, and later in his bed, he wished he hadn't looked down—because what he saw would stay with him for the rest of his life. A hole in the street easily twenty feet deep. At the bottom jagged concrete.

Something had stopped him. Something had saved him from certain death.

Something or someone.

4

Voices

Owen limped home in a daze, trying to make sense of what had happened at the Briarwood Café and over the hole in the ground. He steered clear of the restaurant and listened carefully for any more whispers, but all he heard were crows and a few stray geese.

Yes, Owen had written an article about a recent wrestling tournament for the school newspaper, but he remembered nothing critical of or disparaging about Gordan. True, Owen didn't particularly like Gordan. The very way the big boy carried himself and the gaggle of rowdy friends he attracted made Owen avoid him.

Owen reached the corner near his house and looked both ways. He wondered if Gordan knew about the hole. Was that why he'd stopped chasing him? He and his friends would practice surprised looks and stunned stares for the next day when pressed about Owen's "accident."

Owen scurried across the street and a half block down to his father's bookstore next to the Blackstone Tavern. The Blackstone looked like it had been there since dinosaurs roamed the earth. Owen thought they should serve meals in wooden bowls. On the other side of the bookstore—what was it this week? A music store? No, the strange man with gnarled hands who gave violin lessons to seemingly anyone—that's how bad the noise was—had moved on. This week it was a travel office advertising exotic cruises and tropical vacations.

Down the street a dark figure shifted under a streetlamp and moaned. It was Karl, a man who pestered Owen's father. He smelled like a gutter. There was the clink of a bottle.

Through the front window of the bookstore, Owen saw a light shining at the desk. When he inserted his key to turn the heavy lock, nothing happened. No familiar *ka-klunk* of the bolt disengaging or *whap* of the lock. Owen removed the key and turned the knob. The door was unlocked.

If you found the front door of your home unlocked, you might think nothing of it. You might assume someone in your family had left it open for you. But Owen is not you or me, and that is partly why we are telling his story. For when Owen Reeder came home to an unlocked bookstore, a thousand scenarios flashed through his mind: Three high school wrestlers hiding behind the front desk, waiting to pounce. Robbers in the back room trying to unlock the safe. (Never mind that it had less money than the tip jar at the Blackstone Tavern.) Or perhaps a book his father recently purchased had the middle cut out and a stash of jewels inside or gold coins or a detonation device for a nuclear warhead speeding toward an unknown destination.

The bell above him tinkled (which is to say it jingled, not that it went to the bathroom), and he quickly closed and locked the door and pulled the shade. His heart thudded.

Now to get the full picture of Owen's existence, you must pause to take in his daily surroundings. The window next to the door, the one he had just looked through to see the light on the desk, took up the entire wall and displayed the newest used books and the best sellers to the street. Anyone could see inside through this monstrous window, but still Owen felt compelled to pull the shade on the tiny one on the door.

"Dad?" Owen called. "I'm back."

Through the side hall, near fiction and fantasy, came the strains of classical music his father sometimes played in the mornings when patrons sat by the stone fireplace in worn but comfortable chairs and perused their favorite authors. But his father never played music in the evening when the shop was closed.

No one was pressured to buy in Tattered Treasures. Owen's father seemed to have little business sense; he would sell used books for nearly the same price he bought them. With this approach you would think buyers would flock to the store, but Owen's father's demeanor kept all but the die-hard readers away. His scowl induced children to implant themselves in the backs of their parents' legs. He often said, "Hold their hands" when a family entered. And he snarled when he rang up customers on the cash register, refusing large bills and credit cards.

Owen switched off the music and stood before the fireplace, listening, scanning the dark recesses of the store. Tattered Treasures had two levels. The first consisted of the front room, which held the desk, cash register, displays, and a few shelves. The room carried popular nonfiction books, audiobooks, and a case full of how-to titles like *How to Write a Best Seller, How to Train Your Hamster,* and *How to Make the Perfect Egg-Salad Sandwich.*

The large room with the fireplace and fiction titles ran the length of the store all the way to the restrooms, storage room, and rear exit. On the other side of the store, in an alcove that split from the main section, were history and war titles. You could also find cookbooks in that section as well as art books

filled with paintings and photographs of places Owen knew
he would never visit.

A stairwell opposite the front desk led to the second floor
and children's books of all kinds. There were board books
for the tiny ones (Owen called them "bored" books) and the
classic adventures of Huck Finn, Robinson Crusoe, Alice in
Wonderland, and the like.

To the left, a steep stairway above the fiction titles led to
where Owen and his father lived. The small living room led
to the tiny kitchen, which led to Mr. Reeder's bedroom. At
the back was a bathroom (no shower, just a yellow-ringed tub)
and a minuscule room Owen called his own. It was filled with
a bed, a desk, a dresser, and a shining goldfish bowl with a soli-
tary friend Owen had named Herbert for no particular reason.

On the other side of the second floor in a room rarely
opened lay unsold books. As used books were not returnable
to publishers, these would eventually be thrown out or used
as kindling by the local Boy Scouts. At the back of this room,
under a dusty cover, was the religion section. Owen had found
it while stacking unsold books and had stayed there reading
until the shop closed and his father came looking for him.

"Why are these books hidden back here, Father?" Owen
had said.

His father pressed his lips together. "There's little interest
in this kind of stuff."

"Why?"

His father scowled. "Because people aren't looking for what isn't. They're looking for what is. And what you see is all there is."

Now, puzzled and jumpy in the echoing, seemingly empty old store, Owen could have done a hundred things. He could have watched television. He could have secreted himself in his room with one of the four books he was reading. He could have found some dessert and gone to bed. Instead, he grabbed a poker from the fireplace and tiptoed through every inch of the store, looking for his father or whoever had left the door unlocked. His heart skipped when he heard something in the restrooms, which he was required to clean every few days. Owen found the toilet running and jiggled the handle until it stopped.

He searched every room, upstairs and down, finally returning to the fireplace to replace the poker. Here he felt a draft, unusual because for as long as he had lived in the bookstore—which had been as long as he could remember—the fireplace had not been used. He felt inside the chimney, but the flue was closed.

And this is when Owen's curiosity made things worse. If he had gone to sleep or listened to music or talked on the phone or done his homework or any one of the things people find to do at night, he would not have heard the voices. So faint, so distant, but they wafted through a crack in a stone.

Owen bent close. There were more than two; that was sure. One was high-pitched, another so deep it seemed to rattle the stone. And another was his father's.

Was Owen's father keeping something from him again? Owen had asked numerous times what had happened to his mother. But he had always forgiven his father for never explaining, loving his father anyway because he knew the emptiness he felt without a mother. How must his father feel after losing such a beautiful woman, pictured in those few snapshots he kept in a drawer?

On the evenings his father allowed him to go to the Briarwood Café for dessert, Owen would return to a smell that took several candles or open windows to eliminate. His father had always said Owen was imagining it, but now he had arrived back early because of the chase, only to stumble upon something much more suspicious than a smell.

What if the trips for dessert were encouraged by his father to get him away? Could his father be mixed up in something illegal, dealing drugs or fencing stolen items? What if his father was a terrorist, using the bookstore as a base?

In fact, Owen's father was none of the above.

It was much worse.

5

Blackstone Tavern

Owen mustered the courage to slip out the back of Tattered Treasures and peek through the rear window of Blackstone Tavern. Call him cowardly, but when his mind spun like this, he could barely move.

Blackstone Tavern, a mass of old stone and brick that appeared to be from some other world, actually shared a wall with the bookstore. Noticing his young, wiry friend Petrov peeling potatoes in the kitchen, Owen knocked lightly and entered.

Owen had bumped into Petrov at the Dumpster in the alley one day, and the two had struck up a friendship that seemed to pick up where it had left off, whether it was a week or even a month between conversations. Petrov rarely spoke. He more often grunted or snorted like an animal. When he did speak, he used broken English, but Owen never had a problem understanding him.

"So, father release you from prison—or you escape?"

Owen sat on a stool, tossing a potato from one hand to the other. "It was a daring escape. I had to shoot my way out. Have you seen my father tonight?"

"He don't come here—"

"Doesn't."

"—unless talk to old Sloven."

Mr. Sloven, the owner, bore a considerable belly and a belch that could be heard in three states. If Owen's father knew nothing about making a profit, Mr. Sloven was his opposite. He served drinks in small glasses and concocted meals on tiny plates that made one think he was getting lots of food. But the man didn't like Owen or anyone his age coming into the tavern. Not just because they were too young to drink but also because Mr. Sloven hated children. On that Mr. Sloven and Owen's father seemed to agree.

"I thought I heard my father talking over here," Owen said. "Mind if I look in the basement?"

"Basement?" Petrov dropped his potato peeler. "Sloven find you snooping . . ." He waved a hand. "You go. He catch you, throw brick. Crack head. I watch."

"He wouldn't do that, would he?"

Petrov shook his head. "You teenager. Dance. Go movie. Kiss girl. Basement for hungry animal. Small with big teeth." He lifted his upper lip and showed his decaying teeth.

"I'll bring you back a couple," Owen said, laughing. He patted Petrov on the shoulder. "You can add them to the stew."

"Four in stew already," Petrov said.

The door to the stairs looked a foot thick. Owen left it open an inch so he would have a sliver of light and be able to hear the music and laughter from the bar upstairs. He inched down the crudely hewn rock stairs.

Kegs and bottles and a mountain of flour sacks lay about the room, along with enough dust to choke several hundred rats. Owen imagined them attacking the flour sacks.

At the bottom of the stairs he let his eyes adjust to the darkness. He studied the brick wall, knowing Tattered Treasures was on the other side. Deep red stains marred the bricks, and Owen wondered if that had been caused by wine or something else. The mortar squeezed through the bricks had hardened in grotesque forms, as if whoever had built the wall hadn't cared about looks, just strength.

Owen moved closer to the wall until his ear was pressed against the cool bricks. He listened for voices, but a screech from above startled him, and a furry creature dropped toward his face.

Owen's scream came from deep in his belly and shot up like a geyser. He bolted from the wall, running into a huge sack of flour and spilling it against a wooden beam. The noise upstairs—music and laughter and conversation—died a sudden death.

All Owen heard was a giant creak in the floor overhead. The door at the top of the stairs flew open to reveal the colossal silhouette of Mr. Sloven. His size-17 shoes clomped down the stone steps as Owen quickly brushed flour from his clothes, panting so loud he could barely hear the wheezing man.

Mr. Sloven grabbed Owen by the neck and marched him up the stairs and into the alley. The man used the phrase *your father* a dozen times while Petrov attempted to insert himself into the situation, trying to take the blame for allowing Owen access to the basement. Mr. Sloven wasn't listening, but Petrov's effort showed his heart and how much he cared for the boy.

Owen was wholly unaware that had he been able to stay pressed against the brick wall and listen a few moments more, he would have discovered one more piece to his puzzle. Had he been able to somehow keep his wits about him, he might

have discovered a crack in the mortar that revealed a cavernous room below the bookstore.

◆◆◆

It was in this secret room that Owen's father sat listening to
alarming news: A breach in the carefully guarded connection
between worlds. Grave danger. An ultimatum.

Owen's father listened, nodded, and made mental notes.
Owen's scream had barely made it through the wall, but those
speaking stopped immediately. Fear shone on their faces.

"He must not discover this place," one hissed.

"Keep him occupied," another said.

"Above all, keep him from the book."

"I will," Owen's father said.

"Convince him this world is all there is. Convince him he
is small. That he is less than capable. You know the conse-
quences if you fail."

"I do. I will not fail."

"The Dragon demands it," the first being said, eyes as red as
his master's. "The council has met. This is our opportunity."

6

Small Fears

A person ruled by small fears cannot recognize things that truly
should command his dread. Such was
the case with Owen Reeder as he made
his way to school the next day. The
clouds that seemed to touch the tops
of buildings were gray and lifeless,
making the walk even darker than his
thoughts.

It took dreadfully long to get past
imagining his insides wrapped around
the antennas of teachers' automobiles
or his teeth strung into necklaces worn
by half the wrestling team. Then there
was his science teacher and the alba-
tross that hung on Owen's mind: today
he would have to stand in front of the

class and give his report. Owen had willed it to not be his turn for twenty-three straight days.

If you have not already picked up on this, Owen spent much of his time alone. It was not his choice. His father demanded it, and Owen adapted, as most kids do in circumstances not of their own choosing. Some parents push their children toward sports or music or a thousand other pursuits. Owen's father pushed him to the back of the bookstore, where he stayed and thrived in the pages he discovered.

In a way, the aloneness of Owen's life caused him to find joy in small things. A cup of tea. The smell of old books with, to him, fresh, unread pages. Time to think, imagine, dream. At first he didn't understand why he had to be cooped up while others played outside or went to birthday parties, and he blamed his father. Owen watched from the window as parents in minivans paraded toward soccer fields. But over time, Owen began to feel as if he was not the one missing out. All those children did was obey their coaches and follow wayward soccer balls. One wrong kick and you were heading the other direction, sucking air, and getting yelled at. But Owen felt ruled by books, pages, paragraphs, sentences, words—soaring, he would say, on the wings of writers and their ideas.

Soon Owen stopped comparing his life to those of others and accepted what little love it seemed his father could give. Owen attributed his father's distance to his having lost the love of his life, Owen's mother, so he couldn't fault his father for not showing affection or even speaking kindly. Once someone has lost the love of his life, Owen discovered in books, his outlook on the world and people is often drastically changed. Owen held out hope that his father's story was not yet finished, however, and he hoped the final chapters would be more pleasing than the middle ones.

As Owen neared the school, he wondered whether the whispering voice might return and considered specific bones the three wrestlers might break. Tibia. Fibula. Sternum. Clavicle.

He paused warily at each crosswalk and went out of his way to find the alley with the huge hole. A work crew had strung yellow tape on both sides. His hands sweated and he whistled a Mozart melody, but as the high school came into view, he decided whistling would draw too much attention.

The school was surrounded by a fence—a monstrosity that rose like the silver wings of an ancient bird. The wrestling team usually gathered near the far corner, so Owen went to the other entrance.

He had just reached the door when someone shouted his name. Fortunately, this was not one of the wrestlers.

"Heard what happened last night at the café," Stanley Drones said. Stan was burly with dark brown spots on his face, bigger than freckles, and it appeared that if you could connect the dots you would reveal some picture you couldn't draw freehand. Because of this, Stanley always wore a long-billed cap pulled low over his eyes. He was apparently trying to grow a mustache and beard, but it looked more like peach fuzz. "Close call, huh?"

"How'd you hear?" Owen said.

Stan nodded toward the fence. "Gordan says he didn't think you'd be here today. Something about you running away like a little kid."

Fears, even small ones, sap a man's energy and diminish his strength. As we have said, one of Owen's great strengths was recall. He could scan a room and in one glance memorize people and even what they were wearing. Had he not been afraid of Gordan, spooked by the hole in the ground, or dreading speaking in front of the class—all quite small compared to the evil wings flapping invisibly overhead—Owen would have noticed the grizzled man across the street and the *squeak, squeak, squeak* of the injured grocery cart he pushed.

The man wore a threadbare trench coat pulled tight around his stout frame, his head shrouded by the hood of a bulky sweatshirt. His shoes were thin, a hole working its way through the bottom of one with every step. He sported a gray beard and hair that swept across eyes that seemed alert and intense, betraying the yearning soul of someone in search of something more than another meal.

How much did Owen miss by turning and going into the school? As the tramp saw him, a shaft of light split the clouds and glinted on something golden the man wore on his right hand—a ring? an amulet? The man removed it and placed it in his pocket, smiling.

Above, dark wings flapped.

Watching.

Waiting.

7

Hidden Fears

Lives can turn on simple decisions. If Owen had known what
was brewing, if he had known who
was searching for him and who was
trying to keep him from being found,
he would have been more obsessed
with the rest of his story than he was
with the speech he was to give that
day—or even his issue with Gordan.

Stanley pulled a newspaper from
the bin in the hallway. "Wasn't too
flattering what you put in the sports
section." He read aloud: "'Showing the
arrogance and ego of a more talented
wrestler, Gordan Kalb subdued his

lack of character and decorum every bit as much as he did his opponent, pinning him in record time.'"

Owen turned. "I didn't write that. I wouldn't even know how to write a sentence like that."

"You're the best writer in the paper," Stanley said.

Owen snatched the paper from Stanley. "I'm serious. That's not what I wrote. Some of it is mine—but not this part about how he made weight using laxatives. Who would have changed this? And why?"

Owen wanted to march right into the office of the advisor, Mrs. Rothem, who always had nice things to say about his writing. She was his favorite teacher. She couldn't have set him up. She liked him too much.

Owen watched Stanley disappear into the sea of students, then felt the air gush from his lungs, his shirt yanked tight around his neck. He was dragged into the restroom, and someone stepped in front of the door.

Someone shoved Owen against a tile wall. A fist flew. Soon he was on the floor staring at a pair of shoes in the farthest stall. Converse All Stars.

A foot planted in his stomach. Then against his ribs. He curled into a ball like a grub.

Someone close. Bad breath. "Put anything like that in the paper again and I'll break your fingers."

Another kick. A door swinging shut. People came and went.

Someone over him now. Talking. The assistant principal. "Owen, can you hear me?" He snapped his fingers. "Sit up, son. Can you stand?"

Owen was taken to the nurse's office. Someone placed an ice pack on his eye, but there was nothing they could do for his stomach and chest.

"Who did this to you?" was the repeated question.

The answer was the same each time. He hadn't seen. It had happened too fast. There were no witnesses—at least that could be found in the school.

A female voice. Clara had been running an errand for her teacher and noticed him in the nurse's office. "What happened to you?" she whispered. "Did this happen last night?"

"No, I got away last night, thanks to you. This just happened."

"Who did it?"

Owen frowned.

"I can guess," she said. "You should stay away from those guys."

Owen lay back and closed his eyes, enjoying the perfume that lingered after Clara had gone. His face was afire, but somehow her visit had made the suffering worth it.

"Do you want us to call your father?" the nurse said. "You should have those cuts looked at by a doctor."

"I'll just go home," Owen managed. "It's not far. My dad is busy today with inventory."

Owen limped to the front door, down the stairs, and out the back gate, avoiding, at least for one more day, his speech in science class.

It is this decision that changes our story, for if Owen hadn't been attacked, if he had let the nurse call home, if he had stayed and faced his fear of speaking, or if any of a dozen small choices had not been made, our story might have ended here. But history turns on such chance.

Owen hobbled home defeated, raw from aloneness. Being alone at the bookstore was one thing, but this was a pain so deep that all Owen could do was try to stop his trembling chin and hope his father might say something to ease his suffering. Cuts and bruises would heal, but the turmoil in his heart and mind bubbled and foamed, roiling and boiling as if there was no end to it.

A lesser reader might see this broken, beaten, limping figure and turn to something more pleasant. But not you. You're not one of those who cannot envision any good coming from his story; you realize that every warrior must face defeat and that defeat does not define the warrior any more than words define the heart of a lion.

8

Whispers

What Owen liked most about his favorite books was that they told stories without a lot of boring stuff. And so, in honor of him, that is our aim too.

With everything else that had befallen our hero, should he have been surprised at the freezing rain that blew sideways into his bruised face? He limped under the awning of Tattered Treasures, one eye swollen shut. On the front door a sign read Closed—Will Return after Lunch.

Owen had forgotten his key, but he and his father hid one above the trim over the back door in the alley. He hunched his shoulders against the biting cold and lurched to stand under the awning over the entrance to Blackstone Tavern. He intended to cut through their kitchen to the back, but if he ran into old man Sloven instead of Petrov . . .

Owen skirted the entrance and went all the way around the building and through the alley, the rain freezing him to his freshly injured bones. He located the key and hurried inside, hanging his thin jacket on the back of the door, droplets ticking on the linoleum, gathering in a puddle.

Owen heard a noise. "Dad? I got hurt at school." Without turning on the lights, he entered the long fiction section, past fantasy and mystery to his left, mainstream fiction to his right. He paused at the fireplace, near the tribute to Ernest Hemingway, and listened for voices as he squinted in the darkness to scan the display of Hemingway titles and the pictorial history that showed the novelist holding dead animals in Africa and sitting in some French bistro.

Shivering, Owen gingerly tiptoed upstairs to the kitchen, where he found a package of peas in the freezer. He put this over his swollen eye and moved back downstairs.

Whispers.

Owen stopped dead, a sliver of frost sliding in slow motion off the melting bag to the floor.

Whispers.

In the walls. Behind books. From the rafters.

Owen was glued to the spot near the cash register, as if his feet were in cement. The place, so familiar, felt eerie in the low light. He wished his father were here. He wished anyone were here—even Connie, the little pest who bugged him when her mother brought her to the store. Her real name was Constance, but Owen called her Constant, as in Constant Pain.

He finally forced himself to move into the next room, back to a chair near the fireplace and a picture of Hemingway displaying a fresh-caught fish bigger than Owen. He sat down and laid the pea bag over the arm of the chair, something for which his father would have scolded him. He willed the whispers to go away, but they only grew louder.

Strange. The rug in the corner in front of the biggest bookcase in the store had been pulled back.

Owen grabbed the bag of peas and slid from the chair, whispers surrounding him. He knelt and scooted silently toward a vent in the floor. He put his ear close to the opening and strained, but he could make out only bits and pieces, sentence fragments.

". . . must keep him away . . ."

". . . dangerous to the cause . . ."

". . . never know what could happen . . ."

". . . Master will not like it. . . ."

". . . not accept failure . . ."

It seemed to Owen as if his heart stopped when he heard

his father's voice. He had never heard him like this. The man was usually brusque and dismissive, often harsh. Now he had a whine in his voice and was nearly weeping. "I have done everything you've asked. Why must you torture me like this?"

Owen quietly, painfully stretched out and lay next to the vent, putting the frozen bag to his injured eye. His mind raced—the same way it had when he was younger and he imagined monsters in his room, slithering demons with hideous faces and scaly bodies. He would cower under the covers for what seemed like days before mustering the nerve to reach for the tiny flashlight on his desk. He was sure the monster was waiting to pounce, to bite off his hand as he groped for the light. But it came back whole, along with the flashlight.

In the end, the monster had simply been a cover he had draped over a chair. Its nose was the round arm of the chair. He would leave the light on awhile to settle his mind.

But now, this, this was no imaginary monster. Something was going on somewhere close. Owen had always believed his father was just a grumpy, sad bookstore owner with bad business sense. So what was all this about?

Was his father such a loner because he was a wanted man? Had he once been a spy for some secret government organization, and now they wanted him for one more job?

What if Owen's mother, instead of dying the day Owen was born, had actually been killed in a secret operation to overthrow some dictator, and after that his father had gone into hiding?

What if his father was actually a bank robber? That would explain how he had enough money to buy the bookstore and not care how many books he sold. And what if Owen's mother had been killed assisting some terrorist action?

Suddenly the whispers stopped and footsteps approached.

A draft reached the huge dictionary lying on its side at the end of a shelf, and its thousand pages began to flap, opening to the *D* section. Had you been a fly on the wall, you would have noted that at the top of the page was the word *deathbed* and at the bottom of the next, *deceit*.

Owen quickly became aware of the musty, pungent aroma that had greeted him before, smoky and dank, like something burning. He tried to shut down his breathing and wanted to open a window or a door. But that was impossible, because as much as he abhorred the smell and as much as he wanted to escape, he was transfixed. For at that very moment the huge bookcase in the corner, the only one built into the wall of the old building, moved.

Impossible as it seems, the floor-to-ceiling shelving loaded with the heaviest volumes inched out toward the pulled-back rug, creaking under the weight of all those pages, all those words.

Breath held, heart hammering, Owen silently leaped to his

feet and moved into hiding behind a shelf shrouded in darkness, peering over duplicate copies of *For Whom the Bell Tolls*.

A flame flickered from the dark passage beneath the massive bookshelf, and a puff of dusty air shot from the opening, as if a tent flap had just closed or the wings of some giant bird had just flapped.

Owen stared at the shadows of giant figures reflected on the stone walls as they ascended. Owen's father led the way, followed by three cloaked figures who looked as if they had walked straight out of the third stave of Charles Dickens's *A Christmas Carol,* cousins of the Ghost of Christmas Yet to Come. Owen's father reached high and grasped an ivory bookend in the shape of Medusa, the Greek mythological figure with snakes' heads protruding from her own. With one tug, the bookcase began its slow, groaning close.

The mysterious other three followed Owen's father toward the next room, allowing Owen to breathe. But the last of the intruders, the tallest and leanest, paused before leaving the fiction room. He stopped and tilted his head to inspect the small wet spot on the floor. He ran a pale, skeletal hand across the arm of the chair where Owen had placed the bag of peas. The being lingered, then joined the others. Soon Owen heard the tinkling of the bell over the entrance as the door opened and shut.

In all the stories Owen had read, in all the novels and

short stories about children and their fathers, he had never encountered anything like this.

Anyone else in this situation may have waited until the beings had left and confronted his father, demanding the truth. But Owen is not like other people. He stored this scene in his mind, slipped out the back door, and tossed the bag of frozen peas into the Dumpster. He retraced his steps all the way around the building, made sure the hooded beings were gone, and, seeing the Come In; We're Open sign, reentered.

His father looked up from his desk, clearly startled.

Owen explained what had happened at school, showed his father his scrapes and bruises, and followed him upstairs. No questions about the fight. No calls to the school about protection from bullies.

Though Owen's father had never been what Owen would have called a tender man, he seemed skilled enough in tending to the boy's cuts and scrapes. He searched the freezer, appearing puzzled, and finally placed a handful of ice in a plastic bag. "Put this on your eye and rest in your bedroom."

As Owen left the kitchen he turned to watch his father rub his neck.

He retreated to his room, small and Spartan. His bed was his biggest piece of furniture. In the opposite corner, under a dingy window that looked out on the alley and the Dumpster, stood a small desk with three drawers and just enough space to hold a notebook and an opened book or two.

Owen's closet showed the effects of life without a mother. His clothes were piled high—dirty and clean in an unholy alliance.

His father hired a woman to clean and do laundry once a week—actually the mother of the pest Connie—but Owen did not like her. There was something about her he didn't trust.

He had broached the subject with his father, but his father waved him off. "What is done is done. I hired her, and she will clean."

Still, Owen never let the woman into his room to collect his clothes. On days he knew she would be there, he kept his door locked and the key snugly in his pocket.

Now he kicked off his shoes and curled up atop the covers, the dampness from the rain seeping into his pillow and sheets.

As Owen slept, his face tightened. He thrashed about and mumbled. The school counselor or even his father might have supposed Owen was dreaming of Gordan and the beating, but you know better, don't you? Or maybe you only think you do. For this was no nightmare about what he had just witnessed, though that certainly would have made sense. No, if you could have crawled inside the mind of our young friend, you would have seen something quite different—a recurring nightmare, a dream he had at least once a week. Something he had never told another living soul.

Tendrils of fire grow around him like vines, engulfing him. A young female cries. Through the smoky haze Owen sees terrible red eyes and a dark figure hovering. Wings flap, coaxing the flames higher, forcing thick, black smoke down, choking him. When he can no longer breathe and believes he will be overcome, a blackened hand reaches through the fire. And Owen awakens.

9

Constance

Your dad told my mom somebody beat you up, and I wanted to see," the girl said. She sat at the top of the second-floor stairs, her back flat against the wall, two books open on the floor and a third in her lap. "Your eye must really hurt. Does it?"

"It's okay, Constant," Owen said, shrugging.

"Wow, somebody's really mad at you."

Those who are kind would call Constance loquacious. Those not as concerned about a child's feelings would call her a blabbermouth, a flibbertigibbet, or that girl with diarrhea of the mouth. She was ten, slight of frame—as if a strong gust of wind might blow her down—and had silky brown hair cut short like the pictures of Gretel in the Grimms' fairy tale. Her nose was thin and her mouth unusually small for someone so talkative. Her skin was milky white, except for a spattering of freckles on her cheeks, and her arms were thin and dainty. Her eyes were hazel question marks. Today she wore jeans and a sweater.

As Owen stepped past her and started down the stairs, she stood. "I heard you crying in there. You sure you're all right?"

"I wasn't crying."

"I'm sure of it. Maybe you were having a nightmare. I have funny dreams sometimes, especially when I eat spinach."

"I don't see that it's any of your business. Snooping around listening to people sleep . . . they throw people in jail for less."

"Do they? I've always wondered what it would be like to be thrown in jail. Do they actually pick you up and toss you in, or is it just kind of a shove? They probably could literally toss me in, but someone bigger like you or perhaps your father—I just can't imagine it."

Owen closed his eyes and shook his head, then kept moving.

Constance gathered her books and followed. "What's it like to have a father around all the time? I don't have one, just pictures my mom keeps in a drawer, which is not at all like having a real one, and you, you have one that's actually home all day and not out working at some job where you have to drive a long time and stay until dark and then come home and do the whole thing again. Kids with dads like that hardly ever see them. I think working long hours and not seeing the people you're supposed to love would be dreadful, don't you?"

Owen shrugged. His nap had left him stiff and sorer than ever.

"If you had the choice, would you rather live with your mother or father?"

Owen answered without looking back. "I never met my mother, so I wouldn't know."

"I've never met my father either, but I'd much rather live with him than my mother any day."

Owen turned, sighing and rolling his eyes. "How would you know if you've never seen him? Maybe compared to your father, your mother is a saint."

"I wouldn't know because I've never met a saint. But there's no way my father could be worse than my mother."

Owen had always found Connie inquisitive, but when they reached the shelves she began asking question after question about how books were bought, what sort of people sold them, what they did with the ones no one bought, and on and on.

"I can't imagine how lonely it would be to be a book that no one wants to read," she said. "Just sitting there, getting dusty. Don't you think that would be awful?"

"Sure."

"I'm almost in middle school, you know. I don't suppose you even remember that, being in high school."

"I remember. It wasn't that long ago. Middle school's not bad once you get used to it."

"Neither are braces or an amputated leg, but I wouldn't wish for it."

Owen showed her the unsold-books room, and she ran a finger through the dust. Owen was surprised when a tear made its way down her cheek.

"To think of these just being thrown away and burned," she said.

"It's not like they have souls."

Connie shook her head. "But what must it be like being thrown in the corner when there's so much inside? Books aren't just things; they live and breathe in their own way."

"Constance!" a woman yelled from the stairs.

Connie grabbed one of the condemned tomes and rushed from the room. She returned a second later and looked Owen in the face. "I hope whoever hates you doesn't kill you." She turned and ran for the stairs.

10

Finding Medusa

If you have ever sensed you were
being watched, you know how
Owen felt the rest of that evening. He
stayed in his room after dinner, trying
to read but unable to concentrate. Part
of Owen wanted to believe there was a
good, rational explanation for what he
had seen in the bookstore. But in his
heart he knew better.

Some people have parents who sit
and listen and even suggest answers.
Perhaps you have a wonderful rela-
tionship with your mother or father.
Well, that was not the world of Owen
Reeder, and it never had been. He
couldn't remember when his father
had visited his room, sat on his bed,

and discussed anything that troubled him. They had never talked about girls, sports, or even Owen's homework.

Oh, they'd had talks, but they were all on his father's terms, about what his father wanted to discuss. It was as if by speaking once about something his father was off the hook.

So you can understand why, as alone in the world as Owen felt, he could not bring himself to ask his father about what he had seen. Something deep in his soul, an ache so real it seemed to bore a hole in his heart, told him this was something he had to keep to himself.

His mind bubbled like a simmering stew, and with a healthy amount of fear and dread, Owen waited for his father to fall asleep. The man snored so loudly that at times Owen thought his nose might pop off.

Owen opened his filthy window and cleaned both sides with an old T-shirt. The moon was full, and that somehow comforted him.

From the alley behind Blackstone Tavern, a dark figure looked up at Owen, startling him and making him fall back on the bed. This caused the bed to bump his desk and send his lamp and goldfish bowl crashing to the floor in a shower of glass and water.

"What in the world?" his father cried out, rushing from his room.

"I slipped," Owen said, trying frantically to find his fish.

"Well, clean that up, and don't cut yourself. Then get to bed."

Owen, strangely warmed by his father's seeming concern that he not hurt himself, found pieces of glass near the heating vent and spotted the edge of the fish's orange tail inside. He hurried to the kitchen for a butter knife and pried the vent from the floor, then stuck his arm as far down as he could. But it was too late. Herbert was gone.

When Owen had cleaned up the mess, he looked out the window again. The shadowy figure was gone, but Owen could have sworn he heard chuckling in the alley.

After midnight, with his father snoring away, Owen crept from his room. He shuddered as the floor creaked, but his father only gave a snort, then resumed snoring.

The door to the hallway was locked, and Owen went through the painstaking routine of pulling each latch back as quietly as he could.

When he was finally on the other side of the door and headed downstairs, he could breathe again. He stood by the cash register and listened. Water in pipes. A clock ticking. The hum of the refrigerator. The scratching of mice in the walls.

At times like this Owen wished his father had let him have a dog. He had long dreamed of such a companion, and now with Herbert lost down the heating vent . . .

Owen often made a point of passing the pet shop and looking at the dogs in their cages. He would smile at the pups and imagine one sleeping at the foot of his bed and going on great adventures with him. It's the type of dream boys are supposed to grow out of by high school, but Owen was sure a dog would solve his problems.

Soon, as you might imagine, something as mundane as a dog for a pet would be the last thing on Owen's mind.

He tiptoed into the fiction room, his back to the fireplace, scanning the corner bookcase in the darkness. He pulled the rug away and ran his hand along the inside of the top shelf, feeling for the Medusa bookend, but he couldn't quite reach it. He snatched a rickety chair from behind the cash register and hurried back.

Owen began to wonder if the beating had caused him to imagine the whole thing. He could mix up the world in his mind and what was real, couldn't he? But he had seen the weird visitors and had watched his father lead them from the room.

Owen had not tested the chair before standing on it, and now it shifted and he lost his balance. He grabbed for the shelf and caught hold of the ivory Medusa head.

As he hung there, the chair slammed to the floor. Something creaked, and Owen was sure his father had heard him. But his father still snored, and the creaking was not upstairs.

It was in front of him.

The entire bookshelf moved, and a blast of musty, cold air hit him in the face.

Owen heard a whoosh from below,
as if someone had lit a gas grill.

What would be worse—something
attacking or his father finding him
and banishing him to his room for a
century?

Past the bookshelf flickering torches
lined a narrow, winding staircase.
Owen quickly put the remnants of
the broken chair near the fireplace,
then slowly started down the steps.
He grabbed the first torch for balance,
and the bookcase slowly closed behind
him. Owen felt the sudden urge to
run back upstairs, but as you may have
suspected, despite his slight frame and
seeming timidity, deep inside he bore

the heart of a lion. A lion that did not wish to give speeches before an entire class, perhaps, but a lion nonetheless.

As his eyes adjusted to the dim light, Owen realized that the steps and walls were stone, as if moved from some castle. The torches were spaced about every 20 steps. With his every gingerly taken step, the ceiling sloped, making the passage seem smaller and more closed in. Carvings above him caught his eye, and he tripped on an uneven stair, tumbling all the way to the bottom. Thankfully his face hit dirt instead of concrete, but his bruised eye throbbed again.

He groaned and sighed, then pulled himself up and found a round room with a textured ceiling. A wood table and chairs sat in the middle. The old and chipped table looked like something King Arthur would have used if he'd had Knights of the Rectangle Table. Its legs were as thick as Owen's own, and he was compelled to test its weight by trying to lift it. He couldn't budge it an inch. The chairs were also well made and thick, like the great pews he had seen in picture books upstairs.

Four pewter goblets stood on the table, and Owen gagged when he smelled one. Reddish liquid in the bottom smelled like death itself.

A wall directly across from him looked like the other side of Blackstone Tavern's basement. At either end of the room were darkened tunnels, the sight of which would turn most people away—perhaps even you—but Owen was more than intrigued. His only decision was which tunnel to explore first.

Behind him, near the stairs, another wall was piled high with barrels and wood crates. Any time he thought he saw something move in the shadows, he stood still. When the feeling passed, he continued to explore.

Though his curiosity reached 12 on a scale of 1 to 10, Owen would not go into the tunnels without some sort of light. He stacked a few crates, climbed to one of the torches, and pulled it from its base, which resembled the talons of a great bird.

Carefully making his way down, Owen entered the tunnel to his right, finding the ceiling a foot above his head, high enough for even someone like his father to walk without stooping. The walls bore a swirling design in the blackened rock. The farther he walked, the more an acrid sulfurous stench assaulted him, as if from the very walls.

The floor suddenly sloped down, forcing Owen to slide his hand along the wall—turning it black as if from charcoal. After the winding stairs and the twists and turns in the tunnel, Owen had no idea where he was or which house or store lay above him.

He came to a widening of the tunnel and soggy earth. Then water. Lots of it. Splashing, falling, cascading.

What might be waiting for him? Three cloaked beings had

come from this place; could there be more? A guard dog? A guard wolf? Or some creature with the teeth of a tiger, the scales of a crocodile, and the claws of a bear?

Or what if the shadowy figure in the alley had access to this place?

Owen entered a cave, primitive and natural. Wings flapped overhead and Owen ducked, the reflection of the torchlight flickering eerily on the surface of water. He couldn't believe he had descended so far as to allow a ceiling 50 feet high with stalactites that reached nearly close enough for him to touch.

He stayed back from the edge of the water, for because he had spent most of his life reading, Owen had never learned to swim. He had always wondered whether his mother would have taught him or taken him to swimming lessons.

He shuffled along the wall, holding the torch high to get a better look at the water, which looked more like a river than a pool. Foam moved away from the waterfall and disappeared under stones to his right. Across the water lay a landing of jagged rock and sand, about the width of their kitchen, with a small path leading to the opposite wall. There Owen spotted a round, tunnel-shaped rock bearing an insignia in the shape of a dragon—huge head, long tail, and fire coming from its mouth. Strange to see something so intricately carved in a place that seemed primitive and remote.

Along the bank Owen spotted footprints—but not from human feet. These looked more like the tracks of some huge water animal, perhaps a lizard or an alligator. Owen had never even read of prints this size.

Still waters run deep.

That usually refers to a person of few words who has lots brewing under the surface. Thoughts, feelings, emotions.

But the still waters of underground rivers also run deep, which is to say that you cannot look at the surface and tell how far down the river might go or what might be living under that surface or what may have moved into hiding once it noticed an intruder.

If Owen had nudged a pebble into the water, and if we would have been able to follow that pebble through the foam and the murky darkness, it would have passed several layers of multicolored rock. It would take nearly 30 seconds to pass the rocky inlet where two reptilian eyes stared at the water's surface. Owen had seen no snakes, mice, or rats, and this creature was the reason. It fed on fish and underwater vegetables it could see with its night vision. It also fed on rats, mice, and snakes it found in the tunnel or hiding under crates. Its webbed claws grasped its prey and tore it to bite-size bits. If you could have seen the strength in the muscles of this being and known the ease with which it could move toward the surface with just a swish of its tail, you would have quickly vacated the room and headed for your bed.

The job of this being, known in the nether regions as a Slimesees, was to protect the portal from intruders by any means necessary—teeth, claws, muscle. But this was not just a job to the Slimesees; it was a compulsion and a delight. This amphibious creature enjoyed keeping all life-forms from the portal.

The water rose as if something had passed near the surface, and Owen instinctively backed toward the tunnel, tripping over a pile of things that collapsed on each other. Stones? No. Bones. Skulls, arms, legs, rib cages, and more.

Owen stared, the water now lapping over the edge of the river. He scrambled back into the tunnel, wondering if he had begun something he would regret.

He had made it to the middle of the passageway when he heard the roar of water behind him, as if something had risen from it. He heard dripping and then a pitter-patter, like a dog shaking itself dry.

Owen quickened his pace, the torch flame whipping as he limped. He concentrated on the web prints in the tunnel along with what appeared to be dried slime alongside them. He wanted to stop and inspect the green marks, but exploring time was over. He could come back another time. This whole area felt like a playground—a dreary one, of course, but something new.

Owen reached the main room and the table and chairs and crates and headed for the stairs. But a burst of air blasted from behind him and his torch went out, as did all the other torches up the winding stairway. With the air came the stench of spoiled tomatoes, overripe potatoes, dead fish, and curdled milk. The smell of rotting food almost knocked him over.

Owen stopped and dropped the torch when he heard snorting. A wild hog?

Now he really wished his father had let him have a dog.

♦♦♦

The Slimesees moved on all fours, tongue slithering, tasting and smelling at the same time. Through small, slitted eyes he saw the tracks—something much bigger than mice and rats, perhaps even human. He devoured mice and rats whole, and he had once eaten a cat and worn its fur on his head as if celebrating.

But his favorite meal by far was human. The perfect blend. Not too much bone. Plenty of meat. And no bitter aftertaste.

The Slimesees reared up on his hind legs and, with a powerful burst, blew toward his prey. This would douse the torches and slow the human and cut down on all the screaming and pleading, the tears and the thrashing.

The Slimesees burst into the room, banging into the table and knocking over the chairs, splintering the wood. He snorted and shook his head to get a look at the surroundings.

The crates had been moved. The human had hidden himself there, no doubt. He rolled his eyes. Now he would have to move the crates and drag his meal out by a leg, and there would be more screaming. He sighed. Such a hassle.

He had begun moving the crates one by one, peering into the darkness, when he heard footsteps on the stairs. The only thing more sensitive than a Slimesees's nose was its ears.

He jumped over the scattered crates and slithered up the stairs—running on all fours. He heard heavy breathing and the clunk of the last torch. The doorway was opening.

The Slimesees was flying now, his feet briefly touching the walls, swinging his big body from one torch to another. He could see the top, the open doorway, and a figure moving into the world he had never seen.

✦✦✦

Owen dashed into the room, reaching for the Medusa's head. He jumped, but the shelf was too high. The chair lay in pieces by the fireplace.

The snorting behind him had turned into a low, guttural growl, like a Doberman ready to attack.

Owen stepped onto a shelf, something his father had told him never to do, then up to another—a double infraction—and pulled Medusa's head with all his might.

The bookshelf slowly moved, but the growling was closer and Owen wondered what he had unleashed from that darkened world.

The bookshelf closed with a sudden *ka-thump*, and Owen heard one more growl that stayed with him the rest of the night.

13

Dodging Bullets

You might think a snorting monster
would have been the biggest worry
of Owen's life and that he would cower
under his blankets and sleep away
the terror. But as big as the Slimesees
(though he had still not seen it and did
not, of course, know its name) in his
mind was the giving of his speech in
class the next day.

Oh, the horror of his escape would
be with him always. He wondered if
he would ever again even dare to be in
the same room as the movable bookcase. But in the morning, every eye
would be on him, and his lip would
twitch. Sweat would break out under
his nose, beading up through the tiny

hairs he hoped might one day be a full mustache. And no matter how many times he went or that he didn't drink a thing, he always had to go to the bathroom when it was time to speak.

In fifth grade he and a few others had simply had to stand at the board and do math problems, seeing who could finish first. Owen's hands shook so much that he couldn't write straight, and everyone laughed.

Now he had tossed and turned all night, finally falling asleep just before his alarm went off. He slapped it three times before his father came in, yanked off his covers, and ordered him to get dressed.

"But I'm sick. Uh . . . and I'm still sore from yesterday. Maybe I should stay and—"

"No! Just get up and get going. You're fine."

His father wanted him out of the store! But why? "Dad, I didn't mean to, but I broke that little chair near the cash register."

"What? When?"

"Last night. I couldn't sleep and my eye really hurt, so I went downstairs. I stood on it to—"

"Never go into the store that late! Bad things can happen when you're alone down there. Now get ready!"

What Owen saw in the mirror made his stomach clench. Gordan's pummeling and his falling down the stairs had blackened his eye, and the bruise had spread toward his ear, so he looked like a raccoon or Zorro with half a mask.

Owen made his way to the newspaper office before class.

Jim Videl, the student editor, didn't even look away from his computer screen. He was a persnickety person, as editors will often be, and flitted about the room like an insect on a mission. His allegiance was to the school—that was clear— and pleasing his teachers. "Yes?" he barked.

"I know it was you," Owen said.

"It was me what?"

"Who changed my story."

He spoke as if in some other dimension, eyes still on the screen. "I don't know what you're talking about."

"About the wrestling match. You changed what I wrote about Gordan."

"I'm an editor. I edit. I delete."

"And you added the part about—"

"If you have a problem with me, take it up with Mrs. Rothem. You're her little pet. And if you don't like working—" Jim finally looked at him. "How did *that* happen?"

"It happened because you changed my story."

He looked back at the screen. "I didn't change the sub-stance of the story. Just took out some things and added a little . . . color."

"You added color to my face, Jim."

"Be more careful about what you write," he said.

Owen passed the music room and saw Rollie Cumis at the piano.

"Owen, come here! I've just figured out a new tune. See if you like it."

Rollie played a little, and Owen was amazed. The combination of Rollie's voice and his proficiency at the keyboard was unparalleled at school.

"You're going to win one of those contests on TV," Owen said.

Rollie shook his head and laughed. "With this face? You have to be pretty or handsome to win those contests. I just want to write a song that people will never forget."

"Maybe one day you will," Owen said.

Owen kept his head down much of the day, but he could feel everyone's eyes and hear their whispers. No doubt Gordan had spread the news, proud of himself.

Stan caught up with him at lunch. "Gordan told the principal you slipped in the bathroom and hit your head on the toilet. He said he ran for help."

Owen could only shake his head.

Well, he had one oasis in this desolate desert. No matter

how bad things got, he knew Mrs. Rothem would be there for him. She smiled as he knocked lightly and entered her classroom.

"What frightens you most about your speech?" she said after he had explained the situation.

"Everything," he said, careful to keep his face turned away so she couldn't see his bruise. "I can't breathe. I shake. I'm nervous now just thinking about it."

"I can see that." She laced her fingers and rested her chin on them. "And nothing works? No coping mechanism?"

"I tried thinking about everybody in their underwear; that's supposed to make it easier. But then I picture myself in my underwear, and it gets even worse."

Mrs. Rothem smiled. "The hardest part is just getting up there. Once you get over that hurdle, it's easier."

"But I hate it. I feel like I'm going to die or throw up or throw up and die."

Mrs. Rothem pushed back her chair. "Owen, sometimes the things we find the hardest and most painful are the very things we need to lean into. There may be some great orator hiding inside you, and we'll never know it if you don't try."

"Trust me, there's nothing hiding inside me."

"What in the world happened?" she said, touching his chin and turning his face.

"I fell."

"Owen, don't lie. Not to me."

"It's not a lie. I did fall."

She narrowed her eyes at him.

He knew he had to come clean. "Well, I guess my face was already bruised before that."

"Who did this? Did your father—?"

"No, it was here at school."

"Someone hit you?"

"Mrs. Rothem, I'm not going to get anyone in trouble. Something worse might happen. But could you talk with my science teacher, maybe get my speech postponed a day or two?" Owen pleaded with his eyes. Surely she could see that he would be humiliated, looking like this in front of the class.

"That would only delay the inevitable. Maybe if you were better prepared . . . let's rehearse it right now."

"It's not the words, Mrs. Rothem. I know the words. It's being up there. And looking like this."

She nodded. "I'll talk with him."

Owen felt like he had dodged a bullet as he walked home from school. He even felt light on his feet. He had seen Gordan only once from a distance, and the kid had simply sneered, seeming to enjoy the masterpiece he had painted on Owen's face.

Owen still had six dollars from his failed dessert trip, and in the window of the antique store near his home he saw a sturdy white chair for five dollars.

"Quite a shiner you got there," the proprietor said. He was a white-haired, scattered old man who was always writing something on a pad of paper. When he wasn't doing that, he was reading books or talking about them.

"I just need a chair to replace the one I broke at the store."

The man looked over his thick glasses. "Take that one there. No one's going to buy it."

Owen took the chair, and though the proprietor protested, he left the money on the counter. He carried the chair home and placed it behind the register.

His father looked up from a book. "Is that what took you so long?"

Owen nodded. "It was the least I could do."

His father slapped his book shut and grabbed his jacket, heading for the door. "Watch the store."

If Owen had the same ability we sto-
rytellers (and you, the reader) do—
to rise above the world and look down
on it—he would have seen his father
walk resolutely toward the school
building, a piece of paper crumpled
in his hand. And if Owen could have
backed up time and listened in on the
phone conversation his father had
had with the principal, or gone even
farther back in the day and seen the
being with the skeletal hand speaking quietly to his father, he might not
have stayed behind the cash register as
a woman walked in and asked for the
Shakespeare section.

As it was, Owen was grateful that at least the store was open for business. The idea of being alone in the very building where a ferocious monster had chased him from the depths, well . . .

But if Owen had known what was going on at the school, he would have run there to protest. He would not have been at Tattered Treasures to take the money from the woman purchasing *The Taming of the Shrew* for her daughter, nor would he have seen the man in the long black coat holding the door for her as she walked out.

Owen was busy at the register as the man walked in. Owen couldn't know this for sure, but he assumed they were the only two people in the store—and he was right.

The man seemed to scan the new books, but in reality he stared at Owen through his long gray hair that hung to his shoulders. He also wore a dark hat that cloaked a face sporting a white mustache and beard with whiskers that danced to their own tune and hid the heavy lines of life from cheekbones to chin. He picked up a book, checking the price. His left hand stayed by his side as he walked into the fiction room, then back toward Owen.

Owen shifted in his chair and caught his breath. It was the man from outside his window—the shadowy figure in the alley! Owen prayed they were not alone, but as we have said, they were.

The man seemed to be searching each room.

And he had something under his arm.

Under his coat.

Owen's father had never discussed what he should do if anyone tried to rob him, but Owen had read enough about robberies to know that his life was worth more than a few bills. He would give up the cash if he had to, but still he set his mind on a plan of escape. He could hit the man with an umbrella kept behind the register. He could lure the man to a big stack of books along the side wall and push them down on him. He could lock him in the upstairs back room.

Owen said, "We have some really good books back in that section," pointing him to the fiction room.

But the man held his gaze. Something about his piercing blue eyes startled Owen but strangely not in a bad way. They warmed him like a mug of hot chocolate on a cold day.

"I'm not here to buy a book," the man said softly, clearing his throat. "I'm here to sell one."

"Well, my father is out right now, and he's the one—"

"What happened to your eye?"

The question caught Owen by surprise. "A misunderstanding, I guess."

The man grimaced, as if living Owen's pain. "Would you mind stepping out here for a moment? I want to show you something."

Owen's stomach knotted. This is how it happened in stories. The robber asks you to do something, and the next thing you know you're facedown in a pool of blood and he's going through the cash register. But if Owen refused, the man would know he suspected something. Owen moved around the counter.

"You're limping."

"It happened when I was young. An accident."

The man squinted. "What sort of accident?"

"A fire. My father can tell you. He'll be back any minute, you know."

"Take off your shoe. Let me see your heel."

A bizarre request, but the man said it with such urgency and expectation that Owen felt compelled to obey. He had never shown his scarred foot to anyone other than his father. In gym class he wore pants he could take off over his shoes.

But now Owen kicked off his shoe and sock in one motion. "I was burned here—all the way to the bone. They tried to reconstruct it. It's grotesque, I know."

The man studied the wound and the scar tissue and mumbled.

"I'm sorry?" Owen said.

"Put your shoe back on . . . uh—what is your name?"

Owen told him.

"Well, Owen Reeder, for your courage in showing me something that clearly troubles you, I have a reward. Something I think you will like."

15

The Book

It should be said here that if you ever encounter a stranger (whether he is wearing a long coat or not) who asks you to take off your shoe, you should run screaming and flailing to get help.

But though something was otherworldly about this aged character, Owen felt a certain strange connection with him, a comfort and ability to communicate that he had not enjoyed with any adults other than Mrs. Rothem. When he had his sock back on and his shoe snugly laced, Owen stood and looked the man in the eye.

The moment a future astronomer first recognizes the Big Dipper or a future NASCAR champion sits behind the wheel of a go-kart is not often captured on camera. But because this is our story and we are telling it, we enjoy the privilege of describing the moment Owen Reeder's life was changed forever. We know this moment is pivotal and important because of what happens to him in the future—the things he does, the battles he fights, the courage he summons, the foes he defeats. And it all began bizarrely in the front room of Tattered Treasures.

Some say life cannot be dissected and inspected in such minute detail, that you cannot break someone's experiences into such small bits, that it is the cumulative experience of life that makes up the whole. But those who say that have not met Owen Reeder, have not limped in his shoes, and never saw the book that slipped from under the strange visitor's arm and landed with a whomp on the counter. It seemed to Owen that at that moment a pulse shot through him and through the shelves as well. The other books seemed to move, as if bowing in reverence.

An intricate design like an old coat of arms lay deeply textured in the leather of the book's thick, dark, wine red cover. It depicted a crowned lion with a scepter in his paw. His eyes blazed, and out of his mouth came a sword. Other grand aspects of the cover Owen would notice later, but these were what he noticed first.

The pages were gilded with gold at the top and the bottom

so they glowed even in the dim light of the bookstore. The front edges, however, were pure white, uneven and ragged. It was unlike any book Owen had ever seen, and, as you know, he had seen many.

The very size of the book took Owen's breath, as if the reading of it could take a lifetime. But to him, no book was too long, unless it was boring, and then even if it was short, it was long, if you know what we mean. If a story captured him, he wished it would never end. For instance, he loved *War and Peace* and *Les Misérables*, which each took more than a week and a half to read, even for a speed-reader like Owen.

This thrill inside Owen, this kindling that had long awaited ignition, could not, of course, be seen by the naked eye (or even a clothed one). Not even a surgeon would have seen it in his liver or kidneys or stomach or large intestine or even in his pituitary gland, for it lay somewhere deeper than all this in a place not made of blood or bone or flesh. No, it lay in the deepest place of humanity—where mind, body, and soul connect.

Owen ran a hand over the spine—as thick as three math textbooks—caressing the textured leather. "Some animal gave its life to cover this."

The man chuckled. "Several actually."

"Where did you find it?"

The man leaned against the counter, still holding Owen's gaze. "This book is not found. It finds. It is not simply stories and words; it goes deeper."

"If it's so special, why would you want to sell it?"

The man bit his lip. "Open it. Read it. Try it."

The thick, rich leather squeaked as Owen opened it, and it felt tight and new, as if he might be the first reader. The front matter consisted of a three-sectioned map, one showing mountain ranges, fields, and walled fortresses. The map to the right looked very much like Owen's own community, and above the two was another realm with strange, winged creatures.

So, Owen thought, *this must be a fantasy.* He couldn't wait to dive in, so he turned to the first page.

THE BOOK OF THE KING

By Elias

When the shadows of two worlds collide and the four portals are breached, know that the end of the reign of the evil one is near. Men will bring news of the return of justice and righteousness, along with the return of the Son. What has been two will be made one throughout the land. Make way a path in the wilderness for the Searcher. Open the portal for the Wormling, for he will be armed with the book.

Let there be rejoicing in every hill and valley, from the tops of the mountains to the depths of the oceans. Let every creature that has breath, on earth and under and over, cry out. Victory is at hand. The shadows will be dispelled, and the Son will return for his bride.

Owen trembled as he leafed through the pages. Everywhere he turned, passages read like prophecies, telling the future of some distant land—urging the people to be happy, to look forward to their day of deliverance. Other pages contained warnings or encouragement to do what was right. He could see the tome also contained stories of battles and heroic sacrifices made by warriors. Others appeared to be love stories with heroes rescuing damsels from certain death. Owen didn't want to be rude, but he had become so immediately captivated that he wished he could just go somewhere and curl up by a fire to immerse himself in this treasure.

Toward the back Owen found blank sections where it appeared the reader could jot his own thoughts, but who would write in such a book? Without perfect handwriting and lofty thoughts of deep insight, scribbling here would defile a work of such beauty.

Owen shot a double take at the book when a page seemed to move of its own accord. This was not a shudder due to a draft or breeze but the very rising of a certain section, like something lay beneath the page. Owen lifted the page and looked underneath, but it floated back, as if he had broken a spell.

He closed the book and cradled it to his chest. "Sir, I'm

not sure my father could afford what this book is worth. But if it were in my power, I would trade every volume in the store for it."

The man stared into Owen's eyes. "You have no idea of its true worth. Nor of the danger it presents."

"Danger?"

The man grasped Owen by the shoulders. "In the right hands, this book represents life and health and peace—all that is good in the land I call home. But should this book fall into the wrong hands, if its secrets should be taken to heart by the wrong entities, if it were somehow twisted for another's scheme, its power could be used for the very evil it is meant to overcome."

"I don't understand."

The man's eyes shone. "Have you sensed something lately? felt watched? overheard strange conversations?"

Owen nodded. "Even here, in my own house." Then he felt compelled to blurt, "And the other night, I should have died, should have fallen to my death. But I was saved, plucked out of the air by an unseen arm."

The man smiled. "The power of the King reaches even here. Far beyond the Lowlands."

"King? The author of this book?" Owen's heart was stirred like the churning of the ocean before it unleashes its mighty fury on the shore.

Before the man could answer, Owen's father entered. Owen could immediately tell by the look on his face that his father had done something terrible. But what?

"Yes?" Owen's father said to the man. "May we help you?"

"Father," Owen gushed, "he brought us a book. A magical, wonderful book. I've never seen or read anything like it."

Something passed between Owen's father and the man—words without sound, action without movement. It was clear that Owen's father was repulsed by the man, but Owen had no idea why.

His father reached for the book, but Owen pulled away. "We're not buying books today, Owen. Too much inventory."

"But, Father!"

His father glared like a man possessed. "Enough, Owen. We're not buying any more."

Owen pressed the book even harder to his chest, as if letting it go would be like letting a treasure chest sink in the ocean. "Then let me buy it!" He turned to the man. "Sir, I have money put away—"

"You have nothing," his father snapped.

"I have a dollar left over after buying the chair and a few more dollars I've saved from working here. Plus, I have the coin, the one my mother left me."

"Your mother?" the visitor said.

"She died when I was born. She wanted me to have it—"

"Give me that," Owen's father said, grabbing the book and holding it in front of him. His face turned white, and his mouth dropped open, revealing his darkened teeth.

"Let the boy have it," the visitor said with the authority of an armed regiment. Owen had never heard anyone speak to his father in such a way.

Owen's father stared at the intruder. "He's my son, and I say take this away or I'll burn it."

The man took the book, and Owen's father wiped his hands on his coat as if it had left some residue. The stranger glanced at Owen and seemed to say with his eyes, "I'll make sure you get this book. Someway. Someday."

The visitor leaned close to Mr. Reeder and whispered something Owen could not hear, but whatever it was left his father quaking and looking small and weak.

And with that the stranger left.

What had he said? Owen's father would never tell, of course, but again because this is our story and we are telling it and we want you to know things that even our hero doesn't know, we will tell you. The strange visitor said only two sentences, and they were enough to send a shiver down the back of any man.

"Tell them I have found him. Tell them the battle has begun."

16

All There Is

The bell above the door as the stranger left was the worst sound Owen had ever heard. He wanted to run after him and plead for the book. He had never been as exhilarated in his life as when he had that book open before him. Now he felt as if he had suddenly become a man, sadly watching the visitor walk away.

Owen turned desperately to his father. "Please, it might be worth much more than he's willing to sell it for. You've told me yourself that most people don't know the value of their own property."

Mr. Reeder slumped into his chair

behind the register. "I know books, and that one is worthless. We have too many as it is."

"But you didn't read it. You don't know what it did to me. It was as if something opened a spigot in my heart, and I can't stop the flow."

His father sneered. "You read too much."

"I don't read enough." Owen's world felt empty and cold and small. "I never knew how much I was missing until I saw that book. And I read only a small part. Just think what would happen if—"

"You'd do better to get your mind back on things that matter," his father said. "I went to your school this afternoon. The problem has been solved."

"Gordan? You heard about—?"

"Your problems are bigger than some bully. You'll see."

Owen tried to shift gears, tried to think about school and Gordan and his speech and whatever it was his father was hinting at. But he couldn't. He was overcome by a yearning so strong that he couldn't keep quiet. He had a feeling that book could unlock a door he hadn't even known was there.

"Father, strange things have been happening. I've heard things. Seen things. It's as if my life has some kind of purpose beyond here, beyond anything I've ever imagined."

"You're talking nonsense. That rap on your head's made you a numskull."

"No." And now the thoughts came so rapidly that Owen could not separate the ones he should share with those he shouldn't. The whispers in the night. The voices below. Beings emerging from behind the bookcase. "The other night I was chased by some guys. I ran down a dark alley and suddenly I was stopped, my feet suspended. I looked down and saw a deep hole with concrete at the bottom. I had been saved by something, someone."

His father scowled. "You're talking nonsense."

"I should have been killed, Father, but I wasn't. And I can't help but think—"

"Just thank your lucky stars you weren't killed. I ought to have known better than to let you go out alone—"

"And there was something else—"

"I give you the freedom to enjoy yourself—"

"There was a voice, Father."

"—and what do you do?"

"It whispered to me."

"You mock me!"

"Did you hear me?" Owen was near tears, desperate to share this experience, desperate to be known by his father. "I heard a voice."

"You're demented, hearing things, seeing things, dreaming when you should have your feet planted in reality."

"It said, 'Courage, Owen.' And when that man showed me

the book, I swear to you, every page screamed at me to have courage."

"That's your own mind telling you to quit being afraid of . . . whatever it is you're afraid of. Listen to it."

"No, Father. No. This isn't about courage to face little fears. It's as if I was made for something more, destined for something—something really dangerous." The stranger had warned of the danger of the book.

Owen knelt by his father and touched his arm, but the man pulled back as if Owen's hand were dead or dying. "Father, I believe there is more for me than what I can see here. I don't know what that means, but I think if I have the courage to act on it, it could change my life. It could change *our* lives."

Owen's father's nostrils flared like a wild animal's, and he ran his hands through his thinning hair. "I should never have taken you on."

"Taken me on?"

"This is all there is, Owen," his father spat. "There is nothing more. Do you understand? You have to live for this world, not something you've dreamed or heard from some voice in the night. Clear the cobwebs from your mind and get used to it, child. This is all there is."

17

The Shield

Owen slept fitfully that night, hearing voices and dreaming. The fire. Red eyes watching him.

He awoke with a pain in his foot and nearly cried out, the echo of his father's words in his ears: *This is all there is.*

He thought about all these things on his way to school, but he had no idea his father could be so intrusive, so violating, until he saw Mrs. Rothem's empty desk. Her things were gone.

Owen rushed to the office.

"She's been reassigned to another school," the vice principal said.

Owen could barely catch his breath. "Why? What did she do?"

The man shuffled papers and would not meet Owen's gaze. "Owen, you should get to class."

"Was it my father? What did he say?"

"Hurry. You'll be late."

But Owen did not want to go to class, and he could not imagine a school without Mrs. Rothem. He could picture nothing crueler than his father driving her out. And why would he? Why chase away the one person who had befriended Owen?

Owen could not shake the thoughts of his father's clandestine meetings, the moving bookshelf, the underground caverns, the footprints, the pursuing monster, and then his father's reaction to the strange man and his book. Oh, the feel of that volume in his hands!

As he limped out of the vice principal's office and into the stream of humanity that was his high school, he felt like a stranger, an alien. Was this no longer his world? He ached for the book the way he ached to be held by the mother he had never known. What a feeling of hope the book had given him, encouraging words from his invisible helper.

Why would Owen need courage? And how would anyone know he'd need it?

Owen's mind, as you can tell, was elsewhere, so he had no inkling of the gauntlet ahead of him. They waited like a pack of hungry wolves, ready to pounce. Owen's limp was becoming more pronounced for some reason, his head bobbing, so it was easy for them to spot him in the crowd.

"Reeder!" Gordan said.

When your life is in danger, when there seems no way out, sometimes something primitive, even feral, takes over and gives you superhuman strength. Mothers have been known to lift cars off their trapped children, saving their lives. A rush of adrenaline can turn a wimpy, limping, bookish teenager into a warrior.

We wish we could say this is what happened to Owen— that he slipped off his backpack and swung it as a weapon, fending off his attackers. But in fact, Owen backed away from Gordan right into another wrestling bully, who pushed him into the middle of the hallway. The group took turns spinning him for a better look at his blackened eye.

"Excellent work, Gordan," one said as Owen was pushed against a locker. "Really gave him a good one. Let's do the other."

Owen finally managed, "You know what'll happen if you touch me again."

"Think we're afraid of being expelled?" Gordan said.

"They'll kick you off the wrestling team," Owen said.

Gordan stepped closer. "With all these witnesses? You jumped me, and I had to defend myself, right, boys? I couldn't just let him pummel me with those great big fists."

"He started it, Gordan," someone said.

"I didn't write what you saw in the paper," Owen said. "Somebody changed it to get you mad at me."

Owen noticed Gordan flexing his right fist and ducked just as Gordan swung at him. His knuckles slammed into the locker behind Owen's head, and he yelped as Owen moved to break the gauntlet. He nearly got through, but someone grabbed his backpack at the last second and threw Owen to the ground. The air whooshed out of his lungs, and he lay squirming like a dying cockroach.

And here came Gordan. "It ends here, Reeder."

Owen closed his eyes and braced himself.

You may be hoping the bell will ring or a teacher will appear. Such overwhelming odds seem to demand that someone unseen make his presence known. But let's freeze the punch in midair and remind you of a scene in another book where a teacher answers his followers' question of why a certain man was born blind. Were his parents or the man himself being punished? The wise teacher said the man was blind so a greater purpose might be served, that the work of God might be displayed in his life. The teacher then mixed some of his spit with the dust of the ground and put it on the man's eyes. After he had washed in a nearby pool, the man could miraculously see.

In much the same way, what happened next with Owen

was not for the sake of vengeance, nor was it to bring Owen
or any other creature glory that is due to only one. Rather it
was meant to show Owen he was not alone.

. Because you have graced us with your reading attention for
this long and because we can, allow us to lift the curtain on
the invisible world as Gordan's fist accelerated toward Owen's
jaw. It was inches from bloody contact when everything
stopped.

During that interruption of the passage of time as we humans
know it, a being marched forward and glanced at each combat-
ant, stroking its chin and deliberately assessing the situation.
It moved behind the bullies and inserted an invisible shield
behind each head. It then reached inside Gordan's belt in the
back and yanked Gordan's underwear up six inches, giving him
a royal wedgie.

The being placed another invisible shield in front of each
bully, including one at Gordan's fist, then hovered over Owen
and released the time block, which emitted a crackling sound,
like someone being shocked.

The result was instantaneous. The boys surrounding Owen
flew back against the lockers, the shields preventing them
from hitting too hard. All crumpled to the floor, their faces
pressed against the cold tile.

Gordan's flight was more complicated. He had stooped to
punch Owen, but his fist hit the invisible shield an inch from

Owen's jaw, and he rebounded toward the ceiling. He fell with a thump and tumbled atop a burly friend.

All this happened in less than two seconds.

Owen opened his eyes when no punch landed and caught a glimpse of Gordan falling from the ceiling onto his friend's back and rolling to the floor. The thugs looked like rag dolls, but Owen knew it was only a matter of time before they stirred. He struggled to his feet and hurried off, adjusting his backpack, but as he passed Gordan, the big boy shot out a hand and grabbed Owen's ankle. Owen nearly fell, but something buoyed him. He heard a sickening crackle at his feet, and Gordan released his ankle.

"The book, Owen," someone whispered.

Or was it in his head? "Who are you?" Owen said.

As he started down the hall toward his first class, he heard the voice again. "Find the book."

Owen heard moaning behind him and the sound of tennis shoes on tile—slow at first, then faster. He passed his class-room and limped as fast as he could toward the front door. He hit the push bar at what for him was full speed and raced for the street.

18

The Search

Owen had never been out of school without permission, yet here he was, taking to the streets like the adventurous, curious person he was. He wanted to stash his backpack at home, but his father would be there, forcing him back to school. If he did go back, he would have to answer questions about Gordan and the others, and he didn't know what had happened any more than they did.

He had to find the man with the book, but what if he had already left town? He could be at the antique store that bought old books. The thrift store took in tons of donations each week. Maybe the stranger was there.

As he hurried, he sensed a lighter step. Someone or some-thing was watching out for him, and that felt good. For all he knew, whatever force had whispered in his ear could have an evil agenda too. Perhaps it wanted him to rob a bank. Or assassinate some high official. Owen sensed this wasn't true, but once his mind began working it was difficult to stop.

Walking the streets when he should have been in school was exciting. He felt a sense of freedom, and that made the day brighter and cheerier.

"Hey, Owen!" a voice called from the elementary school playground.

He saw swings, slides, and monkey bars among a grove of pine trees surrounded by a small chain-link fence.

"Owen, over here—it's me!" a girl yelled, waving. Constance.

He rushed over, hoping she wouldn't alert the whole school to his presence.

"Whatcha doin' out of school? Aren't you going today?"

He shook his head.

"Sick?"

"Yeah," he mumbled. "A contagious disease."

"What?"

"I really can't talk right now," he said.

Constance poked her pointed red shoes through the small holes in the fence. "I'm pretty good at climbing over, you know. Got a lot of practice at this place we stayed. An old hotel that was being renovated with a big fence beside it."

"Don't follow me. I just need to think, okay?"

"Two heads are better than one. I've heard people say that."

"Maybe some other time," Owen said as the school bell rang and the kids began to run inside.

Constance moved away from the fence, and he was relieved.

He kept walking, his mind jogged by something Constance had just said. He stopped at the corner and snapped his fingers. "That's it! That's where he has to be."

"Where who has to be?" Constance said.

Owen turned and groaned.

Constance skipped alongside him, her red backpack bouncing. "Where are we going?"

"We?"

"You look lonely. I can help you find whatever it is you're looking for."

"Constance—"

"Connie. My mother calls me Constance when she's mad at me, and I don't really like it."

"Constance, you have to go back. If they find you out here, we'll both be in big trouble. You don't want to get me in trouble, do you?"

Our fates rest in our decisions. Most of us listen to facts and weigh situations, but others act more like stray puppies, following anyone who may have a hint of food on them. These will not turn around and go home, no matter how dangerous the streets become.

Constance was this type, a stray pup whose mission, it seemed, was to complicate Owen's life. For no matter how hard he tried to make her understand, no matter what he said to get her to turn and go back to school, she would not relent.

If he could just find the man with the book and get Constance back to school, everything would be all right.

But as we have said, fates rest in decisions, and Owen had no idea of the ramifications of this one.

19

The B and B

So Owen and his little friend walked along, oblivious to danger.

Owen's mind raced with what might be going on at school: Gordan's shattered hand, his groggy friends, their accusing Owen of attacking them, his skipping school, his missed speech, Mrs. Rothem's "reassignment."

"What are we looking for?" Constance said.

Owen described the man and the book.

"Don't you have enough books in that dreary store?"

A siren warbled over the tops of

houses and stopped before a nearby dress shop. Whatever the trouble was, they appeared to have found it.

Owen tried to explain the appeal of the book.

"So where are we going?" she said.

"There's only one hotel in town."

"Doesn't sound like the type of gentleman who would frequent a hotel. If his clothes are as ragged as you say and he is looking to sell that magical book, perhaps he's found some other place."

Frequent? Perhaps? Owen wondered whether anyone else Constance's age used such words. "Somehow, I don't think he would have sold the book or given it away. It meant too much to him. This is the only place that makes sense."

They reached the hotel as dark clouds moved over the mountain. It had been a cheery morning up to this point, but the swaying trees and upturned leaves signaled a change.

Owen walked into the place—which was shabby compared to hotels you and your family may have visited—but we shall turn our attention to the little girl with the red backpack who waited outside, taking in the sights and sounds. A casual observer might ask why this child would be alone, gazing alternately at the trees and the second floor of the hotel, at the curtains and windows and maid carts with their rolls of toilet tissue and shampoo and soap.

This was one alert child, talkative, inquisitive, bright. Also stubborn, as evidenced by the fact that Owen had ordered her in no uncertain terms to go back to school, and yet here she stood. It is not easy to tell what a child will become, but anyone who gave this one more than a passing glance would have concluded that she would someday be beautiful, intelligent, adventurous, and caring. This last was evidenced in how she knelt to aid a ladybug scrambling up a stalk of grass. Constance let the creature crawl into her hand and travel the length of it and around her fingers. Then she gently deposited it into a crack in the warm concrete.

How much more would she be moved by the plight of a young man in search of not just a book but the very courage he needs to face the greatest evil the world has ever known?

"They haven't seen him," Owen said upon his return, his hands deep in his pockets.

"You don't find good stories," Constance said out of the blue.

Owen didn't understand.

"The book," she said. "You don't find good stories. They find you."

That was what the man had said!

"Maybe you should let the book find you," she said, "rather than the other way around."

Another siren wailed, this time closer, and they walked across the street, looking like brother and sister. The wind picked up, and more clouds blew over. Owen followed the sirens and cut through an alley, moving farther from home and school, as if drawn to something, as if the story was finding him.

The alley was made of brick—loose and difficult to navigate. Constance edged closer. Owen guessed it was because of the darkness and the foreboding trash bins piled high with black bags.

Constance coughed and put her arm over her face. "What's that smell? It's awful."

It was acrid and sharp, like the first strike of a match. A wave of black smoke descended. He'd smelled this before.

"The B and B!" Constance said. "It's burning!"

The B and B had once been a thriving bed-and-breakfast where—before the hotel was built—travelers could find a clean room and a hot meal served family style. But the town expanded, the section where the B and B was located grew older, and homes and businesses there became less desirable. Crime rose, people moved away, the new hotel opened, and the B and B catered to fewer people—many of whom were trying to hide from authorities.

The place was two stories high with a gable on each of its four sides. The roof shingles that remained were dark from the sun and weather, but many had blown away. Paint peeled, and rosebushes and ivy had taken over.

Today a fire engulfed the roof, and flames shot through the

gables. Fire trucks formed a T at the corner, hoses stretched through the yard, and water shot at the flames hissing and smoking. In the distance, thunder rumbled.

Escapees huddled under blankets behind one of the fire trucks. One wore a bathrobe, another was in boxer shorts, and all seemed shaken.

Owen edged closer, listening to a woman talk to a fireman. "There was just this loud sound above us as something crashed into the roof; then came the awful smell and the flames and people screaming."

"And everyone got out?" the fireman said.

"I don't know everybody," she said.

"There was a guy staying on the top floor in that corner," a man said. "Came a couple of weeks ago. Haven't seen him since the explosion."

Someone asked what caused the fire, and the fireman said, "Sounds like lightning."

"But there was no thunder," the woman said.

"This close," the fireman said, "the flash and the thunder come at the same time. Hole up there looks like a classic strike."

"Could that man still be up there?" Constance said, her small voice cutting through the din.

"We can't get in yet, young lady," the fireman said. "That's top priority when we do."

Owen tried to lead Constance away before anyone asked why they weren't in school.

But Constance asked the woman in the robe, "Did the man carry a big book with him?"

"Come to think of it, I did see him with a big red book under his arm the other day. He's a strange-looking bird. Didn't make a lot of eye contact."

"And he stayed up there?" Owen said, pointing.

She nodded.

The black hole in the roof was just above his room.

Owen and Constance wandered a block to an abandoned park and sat on a rickety bench. Branches extended like the arms of a monster. Rusted playground equipment sat unused and weeds grew. The smoke from down the street turned from black to white, meaning the fire had finally been doused.

"Think he's in there?" Constance said.

Owen shrugged. "Someone didn't want him around here anymore."

Constance swung her legs as they watched. "Your father?"

"I don't think he'd go that far."

The rain held off, but the sky remained dark. Owen hoped the firefighters would be done soon. He decided against telling Constance about the voice.

"Ever feel like you're not supposed to be here?" Constance said. "I mean, some people are happy as clams, whatever that means. I don't know if a clam is happy at the bottom of the ocean or wherever they live. I'm happy enough, but part of me feels like I'm supposed to be somewhere else. Doing other things. Or that part of me is in another place, and I'm just hanging here, biding my time. Does that make sense?"

Owen's heart stirred. She made perfect sense. He felt that way all the time—lost though surrounded by the familiar. His life was just a long list of things to do, instead of having a purpose, instead of plugging into whatever it was that he was supposed to plug into.

They wandered back down the street and found yellow tape running around the B and B, but the fire trucks and police cars were gone and the escapees had been evacuated. The sign above the stairway tilted at an odd angle, and a pile of burned furniture and shingles lay by the stairs. The place still smoldered, and it was difficult to get a breath.

"Going in?" Constance said.

"Alone, yeah."

"No way."

Owen turned to her. "I need you to keep watch. Plus, there might be holes in the stairs. Anyway, you don't want to come out smelling like smoke. What would your mom say?"

She tapped her foot. "Five minutes, then I'm coming in."

As Owen walked inside, he put a handkerchief over his nose to filter the smoky haze. The place was eerie enough without the fire damage, but with the electricity off and little light coming from outside, it was downright spooky. Water dripped from the ceiling. The firefighters had torn off the railing at the top, and there were holes in the steps. Owen tested each step, kept to the inside railing, and hugged the wall until he made it to the top.

Upstairs the floors were soaked and pieces of wood and clothing floated. Owen sloshed carefully toward the end of the hall.

Something banged.

Owen caught his breath. "Anyone here? Hello?" He pushed open the door to a bathroom and plaster fell, landing with a splat.

Finally Owen reached the man's room. The door had been torn off and lay on the floor. He stepped inside. The bed was burned to a crisp—Owen could see the springs inside the soggy mattress. The bed seemed too small for a man the size of his visitor. Owen imagined him scrunched up, knees to his chest, cradling the red book, reading it day and night.

A mirror lay broken on the black floor. Owen saw himself in the shards and looked up at a hole in the ceiling that had burned all the way through the attic and out the roof so he could see the dark sky.

He knelt carefully and looked under the bed, then lifted the mattress to see if the book might have been sandwiched between it and the box spring. The charred dresser was empty.

The more Owen studied the room, the more convinced he became that this fire had been carried out with great precision. But why? To kill the man? Why would anyone want such a humble creature dead?

The only other door in the room led to the closet, but Owen hesitated. He had to see what was inside, but he was afraid of what he might find. Could someone be waiting in there even now?

Owen slowly turned the still-warm doorknob and opened the door slowly, causing it to creak. When he had it halfway open, he peered inside, only to jump when someone spoke.

"Find anything?" Constance said.

He whirled. "It hasn't been anywhere near five minutes."

She shrugged. "I don't have a watch and I count fast. What's in here?"

Owen found an old shoe box and a tattered coat. "I haven't seen the book or any evidence of the man."

Constance dropped to her hands and knees near the dresser and examined it. "Sometimes there's a hidden panel in these."

Owen rolled his eyes.

A door banged below, and heavy footsteps echoed on the stairs.

Constance and Owen locked eyes.

20

In the Closet

Every echoing footfall made Owen wonder whether it could be an officer coming for them, someone from one of their schools, or worse. Owen could hardly imagine anything worse than Constance's school realizing they had a girl missing. Owen tried to hold his breath, desperate to not be heard gasping in the burned-out room.

Had Owen been alone, he might have stayed glued to the floor. And had he been reading this story rather than living it, his eyes might not have moved past the last period of the previous chapter. But feeling responsible for Constance, and perhaps with a measure of confidence after what had happened at school, he sprang into action. He seized her hand and pulled her into the closet, leaving the door open an inch.

The footsteps reached the landing, and someone with heavy boots stepped into the room.

Owen leaned toward the opening and heard something heavy being dragged, like the chest of drawers being pulled away from the wall.

Constance drew a breath as if to speak, but Owen clamped a hand over her mouth.

Then silence.

Had they made a noise? given themselves away?

They did not have to wait long to find out and neither will you, for the closet door swept open, and through the haze and smoke and darkness, Owen found himself face-to-face with the stranger he had met at the bookstore.

Constance screamed, and Owen drew her close, assuring her it was all right and not blaming her in the least for crying out at her first glimpse of the craggy face and long gray hair and white beard. As for Owen, a feeling of peace so real he could almost taste it washed over him. Here was the man he had been looking for, and he feared him no more than he feared Constance. It was as if Owen had returned from a long trip and found himself embraced by an entire village. Had you been able to see Owen's expression at that moment, you would have seen his relief mixed with joy.

The man recognized Owen immediately, of course, but looked at Constance quizzically. Then a smile of recognition passed over his face that made Owen wonder if he somehow knew her too.

The man reached in and Constance screamed again, but he gave her what Owen could describe only as a reassuring look. He reached above them, pulled a coat from its blackened hanger, and laid it out on the floor.

"Would you mind?" he said kindly, motioning the two aside. He pulled some kind of tape off the wall, under which he found a small lever. He tripped the lever to reveal a metal door, which he opened wide.

The book!

The man cradled it in his arms, then extended a hand to Constance. "You two shouldn't be here. It's dangerous."

Constance said, "If you avoid the holes in the floor, it's okay."

"I'm not talking about the house," the man said. "I mean—"

Suddenly overhead came a sound that made Owen think of a huge, thick sheet being unfurled in the sky. Or could it have been the flap of enormous wings?

"Run!" the man shouted.

Owen did not have to be told again.

As they bolted from the room and to the stairs, the man pulled Constance while clutching the book to his chest, and another gigantic flap sent a pulse through the house. The whole world seemed engulfed in a shroud of black as deep as the night. More sounds now, guttural, chewing, crunching, like bones being ground to bits.

Owen spotted a flash of red through the hole in the roof. An eye?

"Don't look!" the man yelled, grabbing Owen's collar and yanking him down the stairs.

A sharp intake of breath above, then a rattling cascade, as if someone with a mouthful of water tried to take a breath. A blast of fiery air threw Owen against the man, and they nearly tumbled down the steps. Red and orange flames burst through the hallway, engulfing the stairs and following them as they hurtled down.

The man jumped to the landing, the book in one arm and Constance in the other, as a shape moved past a broken window.

Owen crunched shards of glass underfoot as he caught sight of red eyes watching through the window.

Several more huge flaps, then a gurgling and what sounded like a howl of victory.

"Jump!" the man hollered.

Owen leaped over the banister into the darkness, and his world switched to slow motion while he churned in midair. Behind him came a *click-click-click*, as if razor blades were being struck.

Arms swinging, legs spinning, jacket swirling, Owen free-fell toward the first floor. The wall illuminated red, and Owen watched the man with Constance wrapped under his arm hit and smash through the floor, the wood cracking around them like an eggshell. The two plunged into the darkness, and Owen reached for anything that would stop him from doing the same.

The air was sucked from the room, replaced with a raging inferno. The back of his neck sizzled, and he smelled burning hair as gravity pulled him toward the hole left by the stranger and Constance.

21
Beneath the
B and B

Owen landed on his back in water in the basement, his shirt hissing and his hair smoking. He looked up to a flickering light and realized the floor above him was afire.

The man pulled Owen up, and each took one of Constance's hands. "This way," the man said, and they sloshed through the water.

"Do you have the book?" Owen yelled.

"Don't worry, Owen."

From behind them came a great splintering of wood and a roar as deafening as a lion's and as piercing as a siren's.

The splintering became pounding, like someone driving a tractor down a flight of stairs. Chunks of wood shot through the basement, and a massive, scaly head poked through the floor, nearly reaching the water. But its body was trapped.

"In here!" The man yanked open a small door and shoved Constance in, then crawled in beside her and reached for Owen.

Owen heard gurgling and snorting behind him and dived in, slamming the door shut.

Owen had always feared drowning and was even scared in the bathtub, but he now felt safer half submerged in a foot and a half of water than being grilled like a hot dog—or worse, devoured like one.

When a stream of molten fire filled the room, the stranger said, "Down we go" and prostrated himself in the dirty, icy water.

Constance immediately followed suit, and Owen had no choice either. Immediately the water temperature rose.

Owen held his breath for what seemed an eternity, but as the fire retreated he raised his head, splashed water on the burning door, and kicked it open. He had to dive back in when another wave of flames shot toward them, closing the door just in time.

After the stranger turned a crank on the back wall, a crude

wooden elevator slowly descended. Fire blistered through cracks above them and dribbled atop the elevator. A great roar ripped through the basement, and water cascaded through the shaft.

"He's through the floor!" the man yelled. "Hold on!"

He released the crank, and the elevator plunged and crashed, breaking the door at the bottom. The man shoved Owen and Constance out as the pounding and splashing above them increased. They were just free of the elevator when it was consumed.

"Keep moving!" the man said.

"What is that thing?" Constance wailed, eyes wide.

The man quickly examined the back of Owen's head and his arm. He pulled a small vial from his pocket and applied ointment to burns on Owen's arm and neck. "That, young lady, is your enemy. *Our* enemy. And he will stop at nothing until we're dead."

"Why?" Constance said.

"Later," he said. "We've got to get out of here."

"How?" Owen said. "We can't go back up."

"No, we won't be going back that way."

"Then what way?" Owen said.

The man grabbed a burlap sack, tucked the book inside, and said, "Follow me."

❀

A crowd had gathered outside the B and B, now shrouded in mist and darkness with flickers of light inside. They had heard the commotion and moved toward the yellow tape, only to be repelled by the thundering inside. Somehow the fire had ignited again, though firefighters had declared it extinguished.

When the people heard roaring and crashing inside, they fell back and ran to their homes or any shelter they could find.

After the oily black mist lifted, the yellow tape had melted into a mustardy line surrounding a smoldering shell. The tops of the trees had been burned, and the roof of the B and B lay level with the ground.

Police and firefighters returned, speculating that a gas line must not have been capped. Investigators could not explain the slimy footprints in the bowels of the building or why sharp, pointed scales were embedded in some floorboards. More mysterious, no open gas line was ever found.

❀

Owen feared the beast would follow them, but as they squeezed through a tiny opening and set out through a tunnel beneath the B and B, he knew the passageway would be too small for the creature.

The man found a torch at a bend in the tunnel and illuminated a passage under the streets. Owen was stunned to notice the same strange striations in the rock that he had seen under the bookstore.

After just a few minutes following the stranger, Owen and Constance emerged into a room where they sat on a cool stone bench to catch their breath.

"So it wasn't lightning that caused the fire," Constance said. "It was that, that thing."

The man nodded. "I've eluded him for some time. His desire is to kill and destroy. And his desires rule him." He turned to Owen. "I wish you had never seen him, but you handled yourself well in spite of your injury. How's your foot?"

Owen shrugged. "All right, I guess." It wasn't as if he'd had a choice of how to handle himself. He had simply run for his life.

"Who are you?" Constance said. "What is your name?"

The man smiled sadly. "I am called by many names. Some I would not repeat to one as young as you." He gently patted the burlap sack. "I am a man devoted to this book, so I sup-pose in your world you could call me Mr. Page."

Owen recoiled. *In our world?*

"Is that your real name?" Constance said.

"My real name is unimportant. What is important is that you understand you are both—we are all—in grave danger. Owen, if I am right, it will take more courage than you can possibly imagine to make your world safe again."

"Me? I'm supposed to make it safe?"

"The goal is not only safety but wholeness."

"I'm sorry. I'm not sure I underst—"

"In time," Mr. Page said. "Time and this book will help you gain understanding. It will become clear; I promise you." He stood. "Does any of this look familiar?"

Owen wondered how much he should say in front of Constance. "Tunnels under the bookstore resemble this."

"Tunnels?" Constance said.

"Take that one," Mr. Page said, pointing. "It will lead you home. Be careful of the Slimesees, however. Stay clear of the water—for now."

"Slimesees?" Owen said.

Mr. Page handed the burlap sack to Owen. "Guard this book with your life. If it were to fall into the hands of the evil one . . . It could take you a full day, maybe more, to get through."

"I'm a fast reader, but I think it will take me much longer than that."

Mr. Page smiled and cupped his hand around Owen's chin. Owen had never felt such warmth and acceptance, and he nearly wept.

The man turned to Constance. "As for you, my dear, much is planned as well. While your friend is gone, you must keep the veil tight about you."

"Owen is leaving?"

"He will return. If I ask you to do something for him, would you do it?"

Constance squinted. "I suppose I would. Did you say veil?"

Mr. Page pulled her aside and whispered as Owen opened the sack. Seeing the book in the firelight made it even more wonderful than he remembered. He couldn't wait to read it, eager to see what more lay inside its pages.

22
Through the Bookshelf

W e're not leaving without you,"
Constance said. "Where will
you stay?"

"We have a room at the back of the
store," Owen said. "Sleep with the old
books tonight. My father doesn't have
to know."

Mr. Page's face beamed. "As much
as I'd like to, I can't. It would put you
in more danger."

"You can't go," Constance said. "I
won't let you."

He patted her head. "I'll go as far as
the bookstore with you, but I can't stay."

"You can tell my mom what
happened."

He knelt before Constance. "You mustn't tell her about this. I know it seems cruel to make you keep this a secret, but I have my reasons."

Constance frowned. "She wouldn't believe me anyway."

Owen checked his watch and saw that Constance's school was just letting out. Maybe they could get her back to her house without her mother suspecting anything. Of course, by now the school had likely informed her mother and a search party had been deployed.

When they finally made it to the great room under the bookstore, Mr. Page stared at the massive table and chairs. "They've held meetings here, Owen. Discussing me. Discussing you."

"Why would they discuss Owen?" Constance said.

"Yes," Owen said. "Why would they? And who are they?"

"All in time," Mr. Page said. "You'd better get up there."

"What if there are people in the store?" Owen said. "What if my father is there?"

The splash of water from the tunnel made his question moot.

"About which are you more worried?" Mr. Page said. "People who might see you slip through the bookshelf or being devoured by a Slimesees? He hears us, and he's coming."

The three raced up the stone stairs toward the bookcase. Owen was certain that if the Slimesees overtook them, he would target the youngest and weakest first. Though Owen had considered Constance a pest, he had to admit that her company, her questions, and her spirit had changed their search.

Owen reached the top first and put his ear to the back of the bookshelf. Mr. Page lifted Constance just as the torches blew out.

"Wh-wh-what's a S-Slimesees, anyway?" Constance said.

"A watcher for the other side. A guard of the portals. The invisibles can't be everywhere at once, so they plant these poor creatures—"

A snort and the sound of wet feet slapping the stairs came from below.

Owen found the top torch and pulled. The bookcase moved, and a sliver of light invaded the stairway. Then the shelf stopped, as if snagged on something. The carpet! Owen stepped back and pushed Mr. Page and Constance through, then squeezed through himself.

"Quick!" Owen whispered. "Pull Medusa's head."

As Mr. Page reached for the bookend, Owen pulled the rug free and stared into the empty channel. There, crawling swiftly along the wall, came the monster with green eyes, gills at the side of a humanlike neck, and a mouth like a lizard's with teeth and claws as long and sharp as stilettos. The thing had Owen in its sights, saliva dripping.

The shelf began to close, and Owen stepped back.

The Slimesees pulled his upper lip from his teeth and emitted a hideous growl, crawling to the ceiling, using the slime on its feet for traction.

The door closed just as the Slimesees reached the bookshelf.

Constance stood shivering with her singed and wet backpack still on. Mr. Page looked more ancient than ever, his gray hair and white beard making him appear even more ghostly.

Owen turned slowly, praying no one saw them. Might there be customers reading in the chairs behind them, or would his father be holding a gun on Mr. Page?

The room was dark, as was the rest of the store, but a figure lay on the floor, an arm crooked under his head. It was Karl, the man Owen had seen in the street a few nights before, the one who smelled of strong drink and wore ratty clothes.

Karl squinted with one eye. "Never seen anything like that, Owen."

"Where's my father?"

"Been trying to stay out of his way. Snuck in here to rest while everybody else moved outside to stare at the sky. Something weird going on."

Mr. Page and Owen and Constance moved to the front window. People stood along the street gazing at the sky. Dark clouds churned and surrounded Tattered Treasures.

When Owen spotted his father, he retreated, placing the burlap sack containing the book behind a shelf.

"We need to get you home, young lady," Mr. Page said.

"I'll take her," Owen said. "If that thing is out there, he might be looking for you."

Mr. Page faced Owen. "You must understand that the fight has begun, and we cannot turn back the clock. What has started will be finished, but be certain of this: our fight is not against flesh and blood but against invisible powers that seek to take our very lives."

"And how did I get involved in this? Why me?"

Mr. Page grasped Owen's arms. "We're all in this. It's just that you can see what others can't. You're involved because of who you are and because you have the book."

"Who am I?"

"That you must discover, Owen. Read the book. Follow it with your whole heart. It can change you and the world as well."

A bloodcurdling scream came from the street as a woman pointed toward the sky and people ducked.

Mr. Page pulled from his pocket a knife carved from wood with a blade as long as his palm. "Take off your shoe and sock, Owen."

Owen stepped back, his mind reeling.

"Quickly! We don't have much time."

Owen obeyed.

"What's goin' on over there?" Karl said, sitting up.

"Mind your own business," Mr. Page said. He took out a vial and poured something on Owen's heel. "Constance, turn away. This is going to hurt, Owen, but I have to do it."

An explosion of fire shook the street, and people clambered for cover.

Mr. Page sliced Owen's heel open, blood oozing onto his hand. He pried the coarse skin apart like a pouch, using the knife to press and dig to the bone as Owen turned his face to the ceiling and cried, sucking air through his teeth.

Mr. Page pulled out an oddly shaped stone—or was it a piece of metal?—and stuffed it in his shirt pocket. He tore a piece of cloth from Owen's jacket and dabbed away the blood. From another vial he doused ointment on Owen's wound and pressed his palm there and held it.

"Your wound is your strength, Owen. The very thing that held you back will now propel you toward the truth."

"I don't understand."

"Exit the rear of the store and make sure Constance gets home safely."

"How can he walk when you've just sliced his foot?" Constance asked.

"He cut you, boy?" Karl moved toward them.

Mr. Page held Owen's foot tightly and whispered, "Let the

gauntlet be thrown down now. So that you know what you're up against." He whirled quickly, releasing Owen's foot, and with an expert throw sent the knife straight into Karl's heart. It went clear through him and stuck in a book behind him.

Karl smiled, his mouth twisted with evil, unlike anything Owen had seen. "And now has the Sovereign been brought low," Karl said, his voice different, deeper, almost melodic. "And he shall feel the wrath—"

"Silence!" Mr. Page said. He reached toward Karl. "You will remain in your chains, mute, unable to communicate, until I have gone."

Immediately Karl fell, writhing.

Owen's father burst in, eyes wild, filled with fear. He looked at Constance, then at Owen. At the sight of Mr. Page, he staggered back not in horror but in recognition. As if this were an important person he had seen before and betrayed.

Mr. Page turned to Owen. "Be careful to do everything I have told you. Understand and follow."

Owen nodded, unable to speak.

Mr. Page wiped his bloody hand clean and examined Owen's heel. The scar remained from the fire when he was a child, the fresh scar from the cut also, but the skin had grown together and the blood had stopped. More bizarre, all pain was gone.

Owen's father said, "What have you done to Karl?"

Mr. Page's voice shook with emotion. "I hold no ill will against you. You were but a pawn in this scheme. Today choose what is right and good. Turn from evil and stand aside."

Owen's father stared blankly, as if the words hadn't reached him.

Owen put his sock and shoe back on as Mr. Page rushed out the door.

Another scream. A blast of fire from the sky.

"Upstairs!" Owen's father said. "We must hide!"

Owen grabbed Constance and headed for the alley in the back, snatching the burlap sack from behind the shelf as he ran.

"Stop!" Mr. Reeder said. "Come back!"

23
The Man on the Knoll

Owen and Constance ran into the alley, Owen limping not because of pain but because of history. He had always moved this way. Now each stride freed him from what was known and what always had been. He was discovering a new way. Rather than dodging the trash that littered the alley, he flew over the wet cobblestones, chasing a new idea, a new thought.

The wind swirled Constance's hair as she panted, trying to keep up. She too pursued something she didn't understand but which was as clear to her as her own existence.

In the distance came another blast, like a car exploding, but to see it we must turn our attention from Owen and Constance to the now-deserted street where one man runs in the opposite direction from them.

As we pass the bookstore, glancing inside, we see Owen's father bent over Karl, lying on the floor with his mouth shut tight and his eyes staring. There is something wild and fierce about him, as if he is not a man at all but a being from another world who can absorb a knife through his heart and still live.

The ominous, roiling clouds shroud the hideous monster we glimpsed before—the one pursuing our heroes. Wings flap in the black clouds, air swirls like a tornado, and a howl echoes from the heavens.

Below, a man with blood under his fingernails races through the dark town, trying to elude the flying devil. How he wanted to accompany Owen and Constance. How he wished he could care for them and see them safely to their destination. How he wanted to tell Owen more, to reveal the truth about himself and about Owen and about the adventure ahead. But the man knew the boy needed the truth in bits slowly over time and that the worst thing he could do to Owen was to spill everything at once. That would overwhelm him. No, Owen needed to receive the strength at each leg of his long journey, each confrontation with evil and with truth.

Perhaps it was his mulling over of Owen's situation that

caused the man's fatal mistake. Or perhaps he simply wanted the chase to end because he was old and weary of the battle.

Whatever the reason—and we shall not grant the whole truth of the matter here, for you could not yet comprehend the mixture of sadness and wonder in the man's heart—he slowed as he reached a gravel pathway that led into a wood. He was in the open now, vulnerable, not seeking refuge.

Rather he continued until he came to a knoll, a gentle rise in the earth with tall grass waving in the circular wind, and stood at the top as if simply giving up. As he reached the apex of that knoll, he took off his hat, revealing gray hair. Here was a man of such dignity that he refused to die without facing his enemy.

He knelt and reached into his shirt pocket, producing the object he had removed from Owen's heel, and stretched it toward heaven, lips moving in a wonderful cadence and tears rolling from tired eyes. His hands trembled, his eyes closed, and his heart broke.

The horrible being with red eyes and a taste for blood escaped the darkness and fell like a stone, finally hovering directly over the man. Hatred filled the face of this scaly monster. "You thought you could escape? You thought you could hide them?"

Like a lamb before its shearers is dumb, so the man on the knoll was mute.

"Now you will see the end of it," the beast hissed. "And it will result in my own reign. Putting the book in his hands has sealed his death and with it the death of everything you love."

The man opened his eyes and threw back his head in defiance of the Dragon. He dropped his hands to his sides and braced himself.

As we pull back, grass waving in our wake, we see this ancient struggle with new eyes. Innocence. Goodness. Kindness. All embodied in this one man kneeling on the knoll. Above him, heart dripping with hatred and violence, is the ultimate enemy of goodness.

You may desire to turn from this scene as hideous orange flames burst from the mouth of the beast and consume the man. But linger here we must as the fire purges the earth of this figure.

The Dragon descends to the very top of the knoll, scorching the grass so nothing is left alive on the hallowed spot. And when the fire ends, when the hatred is satisfied—at least for now—the Dragon cackles and rises, cutting through the dark clouds.

24

Home

"You're running faster," Constance said, panting. "Whatever Mr. Page did to your foot helped."

Owen nodded and slowed to a walk. "We can cut through the park to your house."

The sky wasn't as dark now, and there were even patches of sunlight. At the end of one street, Owen pulled Constance under an awning, remaining in the shadows.

"What's wrong?" she said.

"I just want to make sure that thing isn't following us."

Constance leaned against the building, her backpack scrunching. "When

I went to school today, I thought it was going to be just like any other day."

"Well, tomorrow you'll get back in the groove."

"Are you kidding, Owen? How can I go back to school after what we've seen? And Mr. Page said I had to—"

"Listen, you have to pretend none of this happened."

Constance flushed. "Is that what you're going to do, Owen? Just how are we supposed to do that? We were almost killed by a flying, fire-breathing dragon, and you expect me to pretend it was all a dream?"

"Yes, that's exactly what it was. A fantastic dream."

"And what about that?" she said, pointing to the burlap sack. "Just a dream too?"

Owen moved to a trash can and dropped it in. "Yes. Now go home."

"What about Mr. Page? the Slimesees? the tunnels? and that drunk man who survived a knife through his—?"

Owen clamped a hand over her mouth. "Never mention those things again—understand?"

She jerked away. "But there is another kingdom! Mr. Page said so!"

Owen reached for her again.

"Stop!" a voice said from across the street. It was Constance's mother. "You! Owen Reeder! I might have known! You took her? I've got the police looking for her!"

"It was my fault, Mother! He told me not to follow him this morning, but I—"

"Quiet!" the woman shouted. "Get in this house!"

Constance started across the street, then turned. "Please, Owen."

The woman glared. "The police will hear about this, young man! You'd better not have touched her. Taking a girl and staying away all day. Shame!"

"I told her to get back to school, ma'am. Honest I did. She wouldn't listen. She has a mind of her own."

"Tell me about it. Just stay away from my daughter. I don't want to ever see you around here again. Understand?"

Though Owen had issues with Constance and her continual speech, and though she reminded him of the horror they had witnessed, he felt sad leaving her in the clutches of this angry, shrewish woman.

"You'll hear from the police, so go home and stay there." Constance's mother slammed the door.

Owen trudged away, hoping he had convinced Constance that he was no longer interested in the battle. He had been trying only to protect her. If he could make her believe he was disengaging, he could convince anyone.

When he looked back, Constance was watching him from the window. Owen wanted to wave, but he thought better of it. She was already likely getting a tongue-lashing, and he

didn't want to make things worse. He certainly didn't want
her to think he was changing his mind and would pursue this
craziness. He had to keep her from that.

Owen waited until Constance turned from the window;
then he retrieved the burlap sack from the trash can and
broke into a trot. She was right. He was no longer limping.

The question now was, where was he going? Out in the
open the beast could find him. At home his father waited and
soon likely the police. School was no refuge. Mrs. Rothem
was gone, he had skipped, and Gordan and his friends had
probably ratted on him. And who knew where Karl was now?

Owen had never felt like this. For a while he could think
of absolutely nowhere safe to go, but he felt a certain confidence, a zest for life he had never known. His had been a
languorous lifestyle (like a koala on NyQuil). Now Owen felt
more alive than he had in all the rest of his days put together.

He had to return home, if only to pack. But then where
would he go? He had no relatives, no best friend who would
take him in. All he could think of was finding somewhere to
sit and read the book. He had the feeling that no matter how
bad things got, the book would help guide him.

He skirted the main streets, keeping to the alleys. He also
kept an eye on the sky for any sign of the beast. But where
darkness had descended, sunlight now peeked through. The
threat that had hung over the land had lifted, as if a new

power had reclaimed the heavens and drained the clouds dry.

Owen strangely found himself thinking new thoughts. Such as, if there were no clouds, the sun would not seem as bright on cloudless days. And if there were no pain (such as the pain in his heel all those years), there would be no joy from the freedom of pain. And if no freedom for people to do as they pleased, good or evil, no creativity. No songs. No books. And if there were no books, then no knowledge, and if no knowledge, no love, for love is the blend of knowledge and pain and freedom.

When Owen finally reached the intersection across from the bookstore he found that his anxiety over his father—and Karl—had not grown as it might have had he been late any other day. He wasn't sure how he was going to handle his dad, but he believed he could.

But just as he was about to cross the street, he spied Gordan and his crew. Gordan wore a cast on his arm, and Owen could tell by the way the others stretched and shifted that they were sore too.

It was clear they hadn't seen him yet, so he crouched behind a garbage bin. Their voices carried through the alley and bounced off the walls. A sophomore boy Owen recognized joined them. He patted Gordan's shoulder.

Gordan cursed. "Don't ever touch me!"

"Bummer," Sophomore said. "How'd it happen?"

"Just horsing around," Gordan muttered.

"So no state wrestling tournament for you?"

Gordan's tone changed. "We have something to talk about, if you don't mind."

When Sophomore shrugged and walked away, Gordan pushed the others against the building. "Something tells me we shouldn't do this tonight," he said, pacing. "Let's let him think he's safe."

"After what he did?" a wrestler said. "He is safe!"

"That was a fluke," Gordan said. "He's always got his nose in a book. Probably figured out some fancy martial-arts move."

"That made you hit the ceiling?"

"Shut up! If we catch him off guard, we'll have him."

"And how do we do that?"

Gordan glanced both ways. "I'll send a pair of eyes in tonight. Get a layout of the place. Then we'll hit him tomorrow."

Owen sped around the other way, behind the bookstore, and darted into the kitchen of Blackstone Tavern. He was out of breath.

Petrov scraped a knife against his apron. "Missed excitement."

"What's that?" Owen panted.

"Lightning and booms. Your father look for you here."

"I need a favor, Petrov."

"You no go in basement again, right?" He laughed. "Big screams from Sloven to me."

Owen didn't smile. "I need to get to the roof so I can get into my room without anyone seeing."

"Roof? What is matter, Owen?"

"Can you help me?"

Petrov put the knife down and dried his hands. "Trouble?"

"Please, I don't have much time."

"Follow me. Sloven need supplies anyway."

They climbed a narrow flight of stairs that curved and emptied into a long room Owen guessed was for weddings or other gatherings too large for the dining room. Another smaller stairway led to the roof, where Petrov unlocked a door at the top.

Owen stepped out and gazed across the rooftops of the town. "Thank you. I won't forget this."

"You talk crazy. What is matter? You run away? I go with you."

Owen knew no one else who would put their job on the line for him. "Your apartment. Is there room for one more person?"

"One bedroom, but you sleep on couch."

"I might take you up on that." Owen stepped onto the roof.

"Hey," Petrov said, "you no limp no more."

Owen nodded. "Surgery," he said, and he smiled. "See you later."

Owen climbed onto the bookstore roof and used the fire escape to reach his window. He slipped inside on tiptoes and let the burlap sack fall silently onto his bed.

Hearing nothing, he quietly opened his door and crept out to check the living quarters. His father was not there.

Now, where to hide a valuable book?

Owen ventured into the bookstore for supplies, and when he had hidden his treasure, he sneaked to the little alcove that looked down on the first floor. Several customers milled about—more than usual at this time of day. Then he spotted his father with a police officer. Owen moved to where he could hear.

"I told you, he's been at school all day."

"Really?" the officer said. "No one told you he made it there this morning but then left and never returned? And shortly after that a young girl went missing. She's back home now and unharmed, but they were both seen at the B and B today. Inside actually. That's the place that burned to the ground."

"And you believe he would burn down someone's home?"

"It's a bed-and-breakfast, sir."

"I know what it is," his father snapped. "But you can't be serious. He's afraid of his own shadow. Who is spreading these rumors?"

"The girl for one, sir. And bystanders saw him. You must admit it seems suspicious for your son to be there when he should have been at school."

"If it was him."

"Where is the boy now, sir?"

"He hasn't come home from school yet, and frankly I need his help when he does show up."

Someone tapped Owen on the shoulder, and he turned to stare into the eyes of Clara Secrest. Owen put a finger to his lips and held his breath.

The officer said, "Please call as soon as he returns. We need a few words with him."

"What have you done?" Clara whispered.

Owen waved her to the back room. "Don't ever do that, whether I'm wanted by the police or not."

She chuckled. "Have you become a criminal?"

"It's just a misunderstanding. What are you doing here?"

Clara leaned against a desk. "What would be your guess? This is a bookstore, isn't it?"

"This is the room of misfit books," Owen said. "You like fiction? nonfiction? gardening? sewing? We have just about everything." His throat tightened as he realized this had been one of his dreams—to be alone with the most beautiful girl in the school, the town, and for all he was concerned, the country.

Clara moved closer. "You have any books about love?"

"Love?" he said, his voice cracking. "Why, yes, I'm sure we have many. There's a romance section, or in nonfiction there are titles about how to find the love of your life, that type of thing."

Clara smiled, clearly enjoying his discomfort. "How about books about older women falling in love with younger men?"

Owen could evade fire-breathing dragons, so why couldn't he tame his voice now? "I—I'm not sure. I could look . . . after the coast is clear, I mean . . . you know."

Clara tilted her head and ran her tongue across her lips. "You're funny, Owen. What's a guy like you do on a Saturday night?"

"You mean, like tomorrow?"

"Tomorrow would be Saturday, yes. Would you like to go to a movie with me?"

"Wow."

"Is that a yes?"

"I just . . . yeah . . . I mean, if my dad . . . I mean . . . wow."

Clara giggled. "Well, talk to your dad and let me know." She took Owen's hand and wrote her number on his palm. She imitated the officer's voice. "Please call as soon as he returns." She looked up. "And see if you can find a book that would suit me."

"Wait. I don't need to call. I'll meet you at the theater at seven."

No sooner had Clara left than a commotion began below. Scuffling and shuffling and loud voices.

Owen peeked around the edge of the shelves and saw Karl pointing up at him.

25

The Discovery

Karl and Owen's father rushed upstairs, but Owen beat them to his room, locked the door, and flung himself onto his bed.

"Owen," his father said, knocking, "open up. I need to talk with you."

"Tell Karl to go away first!"

"But he is my friend. He only wants what's best."

Yeah, as if a mere human friend could take a knife to the heart. He's probably also the eyes Gordan mentioned. "Then I have nothing to say!"

Whispers, his father saying, "Just go. I'll get back to you." Then footsteps walking away.

"Fine, Owen. Karl's gone."

Owen cautiously opened the door to the anxious face of his father.

The man stepped inside and immediately began pacing, not looking at Owen.

Owen could count on one hand the number of times his father had been in his room other than to order him up and out of bed. Somehow the man must have felt uncomfortable talking, sharing dreams, hurts. Owen longed to know what it had been like when his father discovered his mother was dying, but they never talked about it. If Owen brought it up, his father quickly changed the subject.

They'd never even talked about their future. Was Owen expected to take over the store someday, or might there be something else for him? Perhaps a vacation. A move. Even a day at the beach. Owen had always loved the sound of waves lapping on a shore, but every time he mentioned something like that, his father dismissed it.

Now it was his father who wanted to talk, and the conversation was in Owen's hands. "What happened today, Owen?"

"Happened?"

"I . . . I . . . that's what I want to find out. You took that girl from her school, didn't you? The authorities were here."

"I didn't take her. She followed me on her own. Father, what's going on? Why don't you tell me the real story?"

"I'm trying to get at your story, Son, because you're in serious trouble."

"Tell me about Karl, Dad. What has he been telling you?"

"Karl is just a vagabond; you know that."

"He saw me come out from behind the bookshelf."

"So it is true. You do know. . . ."

"I saw you the other night with those robed people—or creatures. Why would you keep something like that from me?"

Mr. Reeder rubbed his hands. "I told you only as much as I believed you could handle—"

"You told me nothing!"

"Which is exactly what I thought you could handle."

"You don't know me, Father. How could you possibly know what I could handle?"

"Don't talk to me that way!"

Owen shook his head and slumped onto the bed. "I want to understand you, Father. I want to know why you've stayed locked up here, why you keep me locked up here. I want to know what you're afraid of, what makes you happy, if you ever think of Mother, what you remember about her, whether she talked about me, dreamed about our family. But it's like you're a stranger."

"I've stayed here because of you!"

"But why? Secret meetings! Rooms I wasn't supposed to know of! Tunnels! What are you hiding?"

"I've been hiding *you*!" his father spat. He tapped his fore-head. "I know you're not right up there, that things come to your mind and you don't live in the real world. You break from reality. You're a menace to the other children. They're afraid of you. That's why I've kept you here. I've tried to pro-tect you from them, and look what it's gotten me."

"It's not true!" Owen cried. He pointed to his face. "Does this look like anyone's frightened of me? Now I want to know what you—"

Karl moaned from the doorway and walked inside.

"I don't want him in here, Father!"

"Forget him, Owen! And enough talk about me. I want to know what *you* are hiding. Where is the book?"

"Get him out of here, Father!"

Karl dropped clumsily to the floor and looked under Owen's bed.

"It's not here!" Owen said, standing.

Karl lifted the bed, staring Owen down. If that was meant to intimidate, all it did was make Owen resolve he would never let the book fall into the man's hands.

Karl and Mr. Reeder tore out drawers full of clothes, tossed boxes from Owen's closet, stripped the bed, and nearly destroyed his desk. Karl was like a man possessed. Owen loved what he had seen of the book, but what could it possibly con-tain that turned these two into madmen?

When Karl slid the desk chair toward the closet, Owen shouted, "Stop it!"

Karl lifted an eyebrow and climbed onto the chair, reaching to the ceiling. Owen swore the man grew even taller, stretching a good six inches above his normal height. Karl looked as if he were made of rubber. He pushed open a tile leading to the attic, and Owen rushed him, hoping to topple him.

Owen's father caught and held him. "It's all right, Owen. It will all be better after this. You'll see."

"How can you say that, Father? Don't let him take it!"

Karl laughed when he pulled down the burlap sack, dust floating into the room.

"Is this worth abandoning your own flesh and blood?" his father said.

Owen could smell Karl's breath, black and full of death. He lunged for the sack, aware of the man's rotten teeth and sandpapery skin.

Karl yanked the sack away as Owen hit the floor.

"I'm trying to do what is best," his father said as Owen struggled to his feet. "I know you can't see that now, but burning this will save you from a lot of trouble."

Owen's father held him back as Karl left the room and started down the stairs.

Desperate and empowered by an adrenaline rush, Owen

pried himself loose and bounded down the stairs to find Karl
in the fiction room by the fireplace. Karl had tossed the sack
into the fire but held the red book, leafing through its pages.
He looked puzzled, as if trying to decipher hieroglyphics.
Suddenly he ripped out several pages and tossed them into
the fire.

"No!" Owen lunged for them, but Karl stuck out a foot and
shoved him across the room into another bookcase. The pages
crackled in the flames and were soon engulfed. "Please don't!"

Karl ripped out another handful of pages and tossed them in.

Owen's father knelt near him. "The beggar with the book
is dead, consumed by righteous fire. That was the only way to
end this war before it began."

"No!" Owen cried. "You're lying!"

Karl stuffed a single page in his pocket and threw the rest
into the fire.

A deep sadness clouded Owen Reeder's face as the ash and
smoke floated away. He dissolved to the floor, his head buried
in his arms.

"I knew this would never work," Owen's father said to Karl.
"I should never have agreed to it. But I had no choice."

Owen looked up. "Choice about what?"

His father walked from the room, but Owen pursued him.
"How could you destroy what meant so much to me?"

His father shook his head. "I don't understand. I've done

all I could. I've given you every opportunity, and this is how
you repay me?"

Owen's face contorted with emotion, and he ran for the
stairs.

♦♦♦

Mr. Reeder and Karl moved to the Medusa-head bookcase
and stepped inside, activating a device Owen had never seen.
It emitted a sound undetectable by the human ear but warning the Slimesees to stay away. An interpreter with an important message was coming.

♦♦♦

Owen had not gone into his room but had rather run to the
shelves at the rear of the store, edging along the back wall
and into the room of misfit books.

In the corner, from under a large stack, Owen pulled out a
heavy paper bag and tucked it under his arm. He climbed out
the window to the fire escape, running to the top of the stairs
where a backpack lay. He stuffed the bag into his pack and
climbed onto the roof.

The night was clear. And like the traveler with the heavy
pack in *The Pilgrim's Progress* or Huck Finn's voyage down the
Mississippi, Owen began the journey, his first steps alone.

He felt the weight of the book on his back, and a smile

sprang to his face. Owen guessed Karl had kept one page of the burned book to prove to someone it had been destroyed.

That someone would quickly realize the truth. But Owen would be long gone before they came for him again.

26
The Realization

Connie waited until her mother had gone to bed before slipping out the front door. She padded down the stairs in her slippers—pretty, fluffy ones that looked like pink kittens—and crossed the street.

She was at an age where she had begun to notice boys—older ones—and the way their hair looked or the color of their eyes or how their long arms made them look more like apes than teenagers or a hundred other things like long or short fingernails, white teeth, or large ears.

Owen had a dreamy face—soft eyes; a shock of thick, wavy hair that seemed to have a mind of its own;

and a smile that looked genuine, not forced. Constance had watched him every second of their day together and even noticed when he had stepped over a line of ants on the sidewalk. He seemed like the kind of person who would not hurt anyone.

However, her estimation of him had plummeted like a broken-winged bird when he threw the book in the trash. To spend his whole day looking for it and to go through all they had endured because of it and then throw it away had been inconceivable.

But she had also noticed that when Owen talked to her mother, a mischievous glint had appeared in his eyes. And it was then that she had wondered if perhaps Owen was being less than honest about himself. Could he have been doing something for her, placing the precious treasure out of view so that in a sense he was stepping over another line of ants, which happened to be her?

It was unbelievable that she, a mere pimple on the earth's crust as far as most high schoolers were concerned, might be regarded in such a way. A warm breeze lifted her hair and her heart skipped as she reached the trash can, the type with the helmet-looking top and swinging door. She pushed it open and stared into it under the light of a streetlamp.

The trash would not be picked up until dawn, and the can was only half full. Connie reached in and rooted about in the garbage. All she found were a few newspapers, a pop bottle, a banana peel, and two candy wrappers.

She couldn't help but smile. No burlap sack. No book. She was right. Owen had not abandoned the book or the task. He would fulfill his destiny. And if Mr. Page could be believed—and she saw no reason why he shouldn't—Connie had a destiny too.

27

Opening the Tome

Owen was waiting in the shadows when Petrov came home from work.

"Father and you have problem," Petrov said as he unlocked the tiny apartment and pointed Owen to a kitchen chair. "I don't need details. But I warning you, Petrov not good company. Sleep like log." He pulled a juicy hamburger from a stained Blackstone Tavern bag and offered half to Owen.

Owen tried to refuse, though his stomach was empty, but Petrov insisted. Owen devoured it and felt satisfied, not just with the food but also with himself. He was making his own decisions now. He had a friend, shelter, and a book he couldn't wait to read.

Owen was as tired as he had ever been and thus grateful when Petrov built a fire in the fireplace and threw a scratchy blanket over a musty old couch for him.

"Sorry," Petrov said, adding an old, flat pillow, "but I sleep now. Breakfast duty tomorrow."

In the dim light, Owen stretched out. The crackling fire cast weird shadows on the ceiling. Whenever one of the embers popped, Owen jerked to attention, recalling the day. He imagined a winged creature at the window, but it was just the trees moving against a streetlamp in the wind.

Owen pulled a small strap-on light that fit over his head with an elastic band from his backpack. He had bought it at a mountaineering shop, simply thinking it looked cool but having no idea when he would ever use it. Well, here was the perfect opportunity.

Owen placed the band around his head, snuggled under his blanket, and retrieved the brown bag from his backpack. It rattled and he paused as Petrov's bedsprings creaked. The young man was already snoring.

How do we describe this moment of wonder and change? Imagine the first time Michael Jordan dribbled a basketball on a hardwood court. Or when Albert Einstein first studied a list of numbers. Or when Michelangelo first held a paintbrush or imagined what he might do with a church ceiling as his canvas.

Do you have a book you call your own, one that speaks to you as nothing else can? It may be fiction or nonfiction, and each time you look at it something within you stirs and you wonder how such a perfect thing can be held between two covers and be constructed of simple strings of letters. Others may scoff at your chosen book or criticize its simplicity or humor or even the sound of the author's name. But if your heart has truly been touched by it, any criticism of it is lost on you. It has genuinely and irrevocably changed you forever.

That is what happened to Owen that night on the decrepit couch next to the fire in Petrov's hovel. The book had been etched by hand in a long, flowing motion by a master craftsman. The thick pages crinkled richly as they were turned.

THE LOWLANDS AND THE WORMLING

To all Wormlings with the courage to go where duty calls, where friends despair, and where danger lurks. It is a far better thing to risk and fail than to never risk.

WORMLING 1

The time of the Son draws near. When the Wormling has accomplished the breach of the four portals of the Dragon, prepare the way for the armies of the King. Let every kindred, tongue, and tribe of the Lowlands ready themselves for battle, for the time of Great Stirring has begun. And this stirring will lead to the Final Union of the Son and his bride. Rejoice and be exceedingly glad when the signs point to his return.

Owen worked through his fatigue to make sense of these majestic words. Something about the way they were knit moved him and told him something glorious was about to happen.

The idea of a coming battle stirred something within Owen, for he yearned for something great and noble for which to fight. His experience with Gordan had given him a taste of what was to come.

Every word, every sentence, every paragraph made Owen feel as if this was what he had been uniquely prepared for, why he had been born.

And then came the stirring of the creature.

28

Mucker

It began in Owen's peripheral vision on the edge of both his sight and his concentration. Something moved beneath the pages, as he had seen in the bookstore, then appeared at the side. When he glanced over, it stopped, and he was sure he had only imagined it. But no, as he continued to read he noticed another wiggle. The pages themselves seemed to writhe.

Suddenly, a tiny head—a real head with eyes and a mouth and antennae—popped around the corner of the left-hand page and locked eyes with Owen.

Owen recoiled, yelping, his headlamp slipping off and the book falling into the crevasse of the couch. His heart hammered as he listened for Petrov, but he heard only snoring.

The small face had looked like a toy, but it had actually opened its mouth at him, showing sharp, jagged teeth. Owen replaced his headlamp and dug for the book, retrieving it from deep in the couch. He riffled through the pages, telling himself he had been seeing things. There was no evidence of any creature, no tiny face or body.

I had been reading about Wormlings. This is all in my mind.

Still he stood and removed the blanket and pounded his pillow and inspected the couch, taking off the heavy cushions. If there really had been a creature, perhaps it had crawled inside the couch. There were certainly enough holes.

Owen tried to tell himself that he was too tired to read, that he had actually dozed and dreamed this. But it had seemed so real! If there was a wormlike creature in the couch, he certainly didn't want to sleep there. He laid the blanket on the floor near the fireplace, checked his pillow again, and settled down with the book.

At the bottom of one page Owen discovered a passage set apart and written in a weird, slanting motion.

The Mucker will lead the Wormling through the portal, from Highlands to Lowlands or Lowlands to Highlands, fueled by the digestion of information by the Wormling. The Mucker shall not harm

*the Wormling but provide comfort and encourage-
ment through the ordeal. The Wormling shall continue reading, engrossing himself so the Mucker
may grow and progress toward the goal: the
breaching of the portal.*

When the page moved again, Owen held his breath. The
creature was not in the couch but still in the book! And
when the small face reappeared, it seemed to understand what
Owen was reading. It hooked a tiny armlike appendage over
the page, like a driver hangs his arm out a car window, and
looked at Owen, squinting at the light.

For some reason, Owen was less terrified now. The tiny
being's outer covering was milky white and segmented. Finally
it crawled fully onto the page, showing itself three inches long
with tiny arms and two teeny feet that looked like a mole's
paws.

"You're a strange one," Owen whispered.

As if it could hear, it actually smiled.

"You understand me?" Owen said.

The little thing nodded!

"Amazing. So what are you? A Wormling?"

The creature crawled to the middle of the page and
stopped on the word *Mucker*.

"If you're the Mucker, what in the world is a Wormling?"

The Mucker set off across the page, and Owen moved his

hand out of the way. But no matter where Owen moved his hand, the Mucker seemed to pursue it. Finally he stopped and allowed the Mucker to alight on his finger. It crossed its arms and flashed its teeth.

"What?" Owen said.

Mucker tapped Owen's finger.

"I'm a Wormling?"

Mucker nodded.

Now I know I'm dreaming. Owen moved Mucker to the edge of the page and leafed through the book. Mucker seemed to watch in fascination as the pages whipped by, like a kid on the playground awaiting his chance to hop in the jump rope.

Owen stopped at a page with a sketch of the Dragon and Mucker cringed. That was enough for Owen. He turned to the back and the blank pages. "What's supposed to go here, Mucker?"

"Who Owen is talking to?" Petrov said, rubbing his head and yawning.

Owen closed the book, hoping he hadn't squished Mucker. "Sorry. Didn't mean to wake you. Just reading aloud."

"What wrong with couch?"

"A little lumpy is all."

Petrov stepped closer, staring at the book, so Owen slipped it back into his backpack.

Petrov eyed Owen an uncomfortably long time. Maybe it

was Owen's imagination, but Petrov's eyes looked red. Finally Petrov turned and went back to his room without another word.

Owen moved back to the couch and decided he would leave the next morning. But where would he go? He was to see Clara that evening, and he wouldn't miss that, but then what? If he was a Wormling, he should search for the portal. No matter what, he would keep the book—and Mucker—safe.

29

Missing

Owen dreamed of flames and wings and ominous dark figures. In the middle of the night, when the fire was reduced to glowing embers, he dreamed someone was crushing him, trying to squeeze every ounce of breath from him. He awoke caught between the cushions and the back of the couch, covered with crumbs and dust.

When the sun finally streamed through Petrov's apartment, Owen stretched and yawned, his stomach growling. He shook off the dreams, attributing them to the hamburger. Had Mucker also been a dream? Or was his father right? Had Owen broken from reality and entered a mental dungeon of his own making? Now, only a day after what had happened with Mr. Page, it all seemed too fantastic to believe.

He put his hands behind his head and let the sun warm his face. This was his first morning away from home. Soon thoughts of school invaded: his speech, Mrs. Rothem, Gordan, Clara . . .

Suddenly Owen sat straight up. The apartment was quiet. He thrust a hand inside his backpack. The paper bag was empty. He dumped everything else onto the floor. His headlamp clattered, his toothbrush and clothes—everything but the book.

A shadow passed in the kitchen.

"Petrov?" Owen's heart sputtered. His breath came in bursts. He hurried into the kitchen.

"You look for book?" Petrov said, his face blank, his eyes dark and swollen.

"Petrov, what's wrong?"

"They look for you."

"Who?"

"Someone from tavern. See you talk to me. See you go to roof."

"Petrov, what have you done with the book?"

"What is matter, Owen? What you have done?"

"Nothing!" And he poured out the story, details he hadn't wanted to share. But he had to get his book back. "Now, who was looking for me?"

"Strange man. Bad breath. Lives on street—"

"Karl?"

"I don't know name."

Owen described him.

"Yes, that him. He ask if I see you. Say father upset. You in trouble."

Owen shuddered. "Did he ask about the book?"

"Owen, father sick with worry."

"Did Karl ask about the book?"

"I-I said I no see you—"

"Petrov! Did he ask about the book?"

"—I tell him you probably home in bed—"

"The book!" Owen shouted.

"—and he leave!" Petrov seemed exhausted, his eyes red pools, despite the fact that Owen had heard him snoring the night before.

Owen drew close. "Tell me what happened to the book. If I lose that, I can never prove any of this happened. I may never be able to—"

"To what?"

Owen feared he was losing his mind. "I just need the book back. I can't lose it."

"I no take," Petrov said. "I no touch."

30
The Lair

The Dragon flew over his kingdom, licking his wounds after his long search. Half the threat to his dominion was gone, but the other half—the worst half—still thrived, limping through his miserable life.

"The wretched urchin will be better off dead," the Dragon muttered.

The Dragon had been sure the boy was with the grizzled old man when he had burned him from the face of the earth in a two-for-one fire sale. The beacon in the boy's foot confirmed they were together. But no. He had caught only the old man.

The Dragon reached his lair, wings strained from the long flight and blood coursing down one. His crash through the window of the B and B had pierced shards of glass into his leathery skin. But that was nothing compared to the wood splinters he'd picked up breaking through the floor. Had he prepared the floor with another blast of fire he might have been fine, but with the taste of blood in his mouth he could not hold back. The chance to annihilate those two at once, not to mention the bystander—the girl . . .

The minions had come after the onslaught at the B and B, praising him, telling him the victory had been won. They stroked their own egos, wondering which might draw close to him, might become a confidant to the most powerful being in the universe, might one day rise to the council. He slapped them away with a flap of his good wing, then belched a fiery blast that consumed one and sent the rest scurrying.

There was no victory, and there would be no rest until the total threat had been eliminated. He would leave no possibility of escape, no hope of rising from the ashes. Even the death of the boy would not end it. He had to also sever the link to the other world.

The book.

Once it was gone, along with its secret formula for his downfall, only then could he rest.

With a light tap came RHM into the Dragon's chamber.

"Leave me, Mephistopheles," the Dragon said, still reclining.

RHM would have, had it not been for the crumpled paper

in his hand. Others had disobeyed this direct order and had paid for it with their lives, as evidenced by the charred bones on the floor. "A thousand pardons, sire, but I believe you need to see this."

The Dragon clenched his teeth and turned, a rumble gurgling.

"It may have come from the book."

The Dragon sat up. "Where is the book?"

"Destroyed, sire."

The Dragon turned his head and blew a blast of fire against the wall. "I wanted the book brought to me!"

"Our Stalker felt it necessary to destroy it by fire so the boy would not have access."

Blood drained from the Dragon's face. "The boy had it?"

"The old man must have given it to him before his demise," RHM said, bowing and passing the page to the Dragon.

The monster scanned it and closed his eyes. "I've seen this before. I know these words."

"Then the threat is over, Your Majesty?"

The Dragon crumpled the page and tossed it in the air, consuming it with a quick blast from his throat. "Fools. This is not the writing of the enemy. It was from a story written long ago. I recognize the names."

"So the real book—"

"He deceived our Stalker. He knew he would be unable to tell the difference. I underestimated this boy."

"Then the book is still out there."

"He has it," the Dragon roared, pacing. "And he must have been given directions to find this . . . what does he call it?"

"Wormling, sire?"

"Yes. He will go into hiding until he finds this Wormling. The device has been removed from his foot. Use every resource at your disposal. I want the boy found. And I want the book brought to me intact, not a page missing. He will not find this Wormling creature."

"Yes, sire."

"If he gets the book into the wrong hands and this Wormling figures out how to cross over, how to breach the portal, he could get lost in the Lowlands. Imagine trying to find a single Wormling in the midst of that rabble."

"It would be difficult, sire, but we would do it. Dreadwart has volunteered—"

"I don't want a member of the council involved," the Dragon growled. "I want the boy found before he understands, before the prophecy is fulfilled."

"I understand."

"Do you? Do you have any idea what this could mean to your future? my future?"

"I assure you, my liege, every available—"

"And who would *not* be available? This means our very existence, our future!" He drew closer. "Find the boy. Take the book. Bring it to me. And kill the boy."

"But, sire, your agreement—"

"Do you understand?"

"I do, sire," RHM said. "I will personally see to it."

31

Hurry

Owen was unsettled when Petrov left for work. Maybe he should have tested him with a knife, as Mr. Page had with Karl. Could Petrov be in league with the beast? If he was, Owen's father would already know everything and likely be on his way.

Owen frantically searched Petrov's room. Nothing.

He was throwing things into his backpack when he heard the voice that always sent a shiver down his spine.

"Look above the fireplace. Hurry. You must leave soon."

Owen stood quickly. "Who are you?"

The fireplace was made of stones

placed haphazardly between globs of cement. Owen tapped all the stones until he heard a hollow sound. He pushed, then pulled a piece of concrete sticking out between the stones. A section two feet long and a foot tall moved.

That's when Owen heard footsteps on the stairs outside.

♦♦♦

Thick black clouds were rolling in as three men hurried up the steps. One was balding, thin, and out of breath. Mr. Reeder. Another was younger and seemed to know the stairs, skirting one that had splintered. Petrov. The third glided up behind them, rising like smoke. Karl.

"I want to tell you last night," Petrov said, "but I afraid he run. Better he sleep, then I bring you here."

"You did fine," Mr. Reeder said.

Karl nudged Mr. Reeder. "The book?"

"Yes, tell me about the book. Did he have it?"

"I hide. I show you."

"His mind makes him latch onto things like this," Mr. Reeder said. "He throws himself into stories and believes he can . . . well, that he can actually insert himself into them. I once caught him making a raft from broomsticks. He said he was going to float down the Mississippi and save Huck and Jim. I thought it was funny at the time, but I'm afraid his mind is going."

Petrov inserted his key, but Karl pushed past him and rushed in.

"Owen?" Mr. Reeder called.

Karl hissed, "The book, Petrov. Where?"

Petrov moved to the fireplace and pulled out the secret compartment. "I put here!" he said, gasping. "Last night while Owen sleep."

Karl grabbed Petrov by the shirt. "Then where is it?"

"I don't know. Backpack gone. Shoes too. Everything."

Mr. Reeder shook his head and scanned the place. When his back was turned, Karl started a fire on the floor. "He won't be sleeping here tonight. Nobody will."

32

Two Worlds

Owen slouched in a booth in the rear of a restaurant, his back to the door. He slathered a bagel with enough butter and jelly to keep his stomach full for the rest of the day.

"You can't stay here forever," the waitress said, a hand on her hip. "I gotta keep turning this table to make money."

"Maybe I'll try some coffee," Owen said. He had always loved the smell but could never stomach the taste.

The waitress poured a cup and stared at him, nudging the bill closer.

"I won't be much longer," Owen said, checking his watch.

He wanted to open the book right there, but what if someone recognized him and he had to run?

A round-faced man with a ketchup-stained tie tapped Owen's table. The man's jowls jiggled when he knelt next to Owen. "Florence says you've been here awhile," the man whispered. "Don't you have something to do, somewhere to go?"

"All right, I'm going."

Owen retreated to the public library, descending to the basement and locking himself in a windowless reading room. It was not as comfortable as the bookstore or his bedroom, but safety was all he cared about now.

He placed the book on the table and ran his hands across the leather surface, shuddering. He opened to a random page, and his eyes lit on a passage.

> If you listen to my words and are careful to follow them, you will find life. When those who seek your life are close, when the evil one wants to devour you, cling to my words and you will be delivered.

Owen couldn't believe that no matter where he turned in the book, it seemed to speak directly to him.

> Two worlds exist as well as the invisible. Courage is needed if the two are to become one. To breach the portal and begin the union, the Mucker leads as the Wormling reads. Intake for both must be continuous to avoid suf-

focation and death. The one who attempts great things shall be rewarded.

As Owen read, Mucker wriggled from between the pages, squirming into the light. Owen reached to hold him. Mucker stretched and yawned, as if he'd been asleep for a hundred years. Owen found it strange that he could be so warmed by this creature, and he had to wonder if his father was right—maybe he was demented and had invented all this in his damaged brain.

Overwhelmed, Owen read until he was tired, then lay on the floor, curled into a ball, and slept.

Clara Secrest stood outside the theater in jeans and a jacket, scanning the street. She had called Owen, but a mean-sounding man demanded to know who she was and said Owen wasn't home.

A movie poster caught her eye. It showed a strong man with long hair, face turned toward the sun, shirt torn from battle, and by his side a beautiful young woman, scarred by something deeper than war.

As Clara studied this, a pudgy young man smacking gum and smelling of popcorn handed her a piece of paper. "Some guy told me to give this to you."

It was a note with a bill in it large enough to cover her ticket.

Clara,
Choose your movie and I'll meet you inside.
Owen

✦

Owen found Clara in the "handsome man" movie and carefully moved down the row. When he sat, he handed her a carnation and a book he had found for her.

She tucked the book in her purse and sniffed the carnation. "Your limp is gone," she whispered.

He merely nodded. He was so weary and yet so glad to be with her. "Thanks for thinking of this."

"I'm glad it worked out. I called and your father—I guess it was your father—said you were out."

"Stayed at a friend's house last night." Owen looked closely at Clara, hoping he could trust her. "I'm going through a big change."

"Change?"

"I guess you could call it a new direction. I've found something—"

Clara held up a hand. "Tell me you're not one of those religious crazies who go door-to-door and beat you over the head with their truth."

Owen smiled and shook his head.

"Or the ones who think you're evil and burn down your house. You see what happened at the B and B yesterday?"

"Yeah, it was awful."

"So you're changing," she said. "Tell me. Tell me everything."

♦♦♦

In the next theater, four boys scanned the seats. "She's not here," one said.

"Maybe she chickened out," another said. "Wouldn't blame her. Who'd want to meet that loser?"

"Shh," someone hissed.

"Come on," Gordan said. "There's one more theater."

34

Secret

Owen spoke as if his words were taffy he was pulling from his teeth. "I feel as if . . . I've discovered my destiny . . . or part of it. . . . I mean, you know. . . ." He glanced into Clara's eyes, wondering why he felt so free to be open with her when he hardly knew her. He was enamored with her, of course, but did that mean he could trust her with things so personal? "It's as if I'm beginning to see how my life fits into the whole picture."

"And what picture is that?"

Owen scooted forward and faced her. "I've been reading a book."

"No kidding."

He smiled. "Nothing new there,

I know. But this one is different. It's like it was written just for me. It teaches that everyone has a purpose, something we were made to do, and whatever task or duty we're given is only another piece of the puzzle."

Clara seemed to study him. "Puzzle," she said, as if testing the word. "And no one else in the world can do what you're supposed to do?"

"I'm not sure. Maybe. But it makes me think that if everyone finds their purpose in life, then everything will come together and fit perfectly."

"And if we don't?"

Owen frowned. "Then, like now, people just do whatever makes them feel good. There's no real happiness or joy. We simply exist."

Clara got a far-off look. "Your theory presumes someone is arranging the puzzle."

Owen nodded. "And you don't think that could be?"

She sighed and shrugged. "It's just that life doesn't make much sense. Maybe I should read that book of yours."

"I'd love to show it to you someday. But I'm on my way somewhere."

"A trip? Where?"

He sat back and closed his eyes. "I'm not really sure. It's just something I know I have to do. The world seems a lot bigger to me now that I'm away from home."

"You're talking in riddles, Owen. What do you mean, away from home?"

"Clara, things are going on that I can't explain. But I know what I'm doing is right."

The room darkened and trailers for future movies began. This was one of his favorite parts. Owen had only been to movies alone, but here he sat, next to a beautiful girl.

Latecomers caused a shaft of light to hit the screen, and shadows moved across it.

Clara leaned close and whispered, "Owen, I need to tell you something. Something I need to confess."

"Confess? What—?"

"Just listen. We don't have much time. I was the one who changed your story, the one about Gordan. I was the reason he was so mad at you."

"You?"

"I hate him, Owen. I can't stand him or the creeps he surrounds himself with. Your editor had already approved and finalized it. When she left, I pulled up your story and changed a few things."

Owen stared at her.

"Listen, when you confronted Jen, she figured out that I was the one and told Gordan. He threatened to hurt me—or you—if I didn't agree to spy on you at the bookstore and tell them where you'd be tonight—"

So it wasn't Karl. . . .

"There!" someone yelled.

Clara grabbed Owen's arm and pulled him toward the end of the row.

"That way!" Gordan shouted in the darkness.

If the others in that theater had known what was at stake and how even their lives would be affected by the fight that was about to begin, they would have been more interested in what happened to our hero than what was on the screen.

As for Owen, he was too shocked by Clara's confession to think clearly. That she had been the one to alter his story was one thing, but that she had set him up was almost too much to bear.

"I'm sorry, Owen," she said, gasping as they burst out the back door. "He threatened me and I was scared."

"So you just gave me up?"

"I'm sorry, Owen!"

They ran for the stairs, but three wrestlers waited at the bottom.

"Got them, Gordan!" one yelled.

Owen and Clara were surrounded, and Gordan pushed his way through the gauntlet, obviously seething.

"Gordan, please," Clara said. "You know the story was my fault."

"It's a little late for that," Owen said, glaring at her. "You told me you'd always wanted to date a freshman."

The other guys laughed, but strangely they held back. They seemed wary, even afraid.

Owen realized that whatever had happened in the hallway, these guys were afraid of him, worried it might happen again. He decided to take the offensive. "Nice cast, Gordan. Pretty. You want another the same color?"

Owen moved quickly toward Gordan, and the bully stepped back. When the others did the same, Owen felt power surge through him. "Join your friends," he spat at Clara, winking at the same time. "You've delivered your prize to them." He yanked her toward them.

The boys parted for her.

"Go!" Owen yelled, and Clara ran until she disappeared around the corner. Owen had allowed Clara to escape and isolated himself against the enemy.

Gordan flushed, as if realizing he had been duped. "What have you got under your jacket, pip-squeak?"

"Maybe what broke your wrist yesterday. Or what knocked the rest of your crew to the floor. Should I do it again?"

Gordan pulled a knife from his pocket and flicked it open. "When I get done with you, Reeder, not a kid in school will recognize you."

"Facial surgery time," someone said.

"This is your idea of a fair fight?" Owen said. "I'm unarmed and alone."

Owen tested the strap on his backpack as Gordan stepped forward. Owen spun and charged up the stairs that overlooked an alley. It was dark, but a flickering light below illuminated a Dumpster filled with black trash bags.

Owen had two choices—neither good. He could stand his ground and face Gordan and his friends, or he could barrel down the stairs, hoping to blast through them.

One more option came to him. He could overcome his abject fear of heights and plunge into the darkness. He held the railing with one hand and protected the book with the other, and as the maniacs charged him, Owen leaped for the center of the trash bin.

Owen had miscalculated. He was headed for the edge of the metal bin, which could take off his head, and if he missed, the street was a poor second choice.

♦♦♦

Gordan reached the top and caught himself just as Owen left the railing. The boy looked like a doll falling, and Gordan immediately realized that Owen was going to crash. Gordan's troubles would be over. Owen had jumped of his own free will, and neither Gordan nor any of his friends would have to answer for his demise.

But just as Owen was about to kill himself on the edge of the trash bin, his body flipped and switched direction by five feet.

Five feet!

It was the difference between a smashed pumpkin with seeds all over the ground and a whole pumpkin plopping harmlessly onto trash bags full of popcorn.

"Did you see that?" Gordan said.

"How'd he do that?" someone said.

Owen wriggled to the edge of the bin and jumped to the ground.

"We'll get you, Reeder!" Gordan snarled.

Owen ran off into the darkness, his backpack bouncing.

35

The Departure

Let us be clear. Owen Reeder was no longer afraid, despite the fact that he had found a hiding place at the back of a Laundromat. He knew where he had to go. But he also knew many people might still be looking for him. Gordan. The police. His father. Karl.

Grateful for time alone with *The Book of the King*, Owen began to read.

Nothing good is ever easy.

It seemed everywhere Owen turned in this book, something pithy perfectly described his experience. He had not come to any of the stories yet, just guidelines for life and wise sayings, all of which seemed to stoke the fire in his soul.

> *Allow your heart the freedom it craves and then have the courage to follow it.*

And just as Owen was thinking of Clara, how she had betrayed him and yet how much he still cared for her and was attracted to her, he came across this sentence:

> *A friend loves through thick and thin, in every circumstance, even when difficult.*

Owen wished he could talk with her again—wished they could have actually watched the movie and shared a treat afterward. Perhaps when he returned.

> *Good things happen on Sunday mornings.*

That had never been true in Owen's life, but somehow he believed it now. And tomorrow was Sunday. Part of him wanted to run from life, from his problems, troubles, speeches, bullies, and all the rest. But deep down Owen knew that the course he was on wasn't taking him *away* from anything but rather *to* something. He didn't know where he was going, but he knew he had to go.

Owen had no idea what lay on the other side of the portal, but he felt drawn there anyway. He put the book back in his backpack and paused, pulling out a small oval frame he had kept since he was a child. In it was a photo of his mother, glum and subdued in an ornate chair, her hair pulled atop her head in a bun. She wore a checkered dress and a pendant around her neck. Owen didn't think he looked much like her. She was beautiful, and he had always considered himself, well, gangly and ugly.

Owen hurried toward the bookstore. It was late now, almost midnight, and his father would be asleep. At least, that's what he hoped as he slipped his key into the massive keyhole and stepped inside the store. He tiptoed toward the fiction room but stopped when he heard a creak behind him. He turned slowly, the hair on the back of his neck rising, and saw someone sitting in the darkness.

"I've been waiting for you," his father said. "I knew you'd come back when you mustered the nerve." He leaned forward and flicked on the dusty desk lamp.

Owen flinched. His father looked years older, frail, his hair grayer and his voice weak, fearful.

"Don't be frightened, Owen. I knew this day would come. It had to. I just wished it never would."

"What's wrong with you, Father?"

"Nothing that hasn't been wrong from the start."

"I didn't mean to hurt you. I didn't want to run, but—"

"You were right to run. If you'd have stayed here, you'd have lost the book." He waved. "I know you have it with you. But before you go, I need to give you another." The man stood and hobbled toward Owen, making the boy look over his shoulder for Karl. "It's all right. Take this. You should know the truth."

"About what?"

"About everything. I am told the book you were given explains much. But it does not divulge the secret contained in this book."

Owen rubbed a hand over the slick surface. "It's just pictures."

The man's eyes closed in a long blink, and he sighed. "I have tried to love you, Owen, or at least to pretend I did. I don't suppose I succeeded, did I?"

Emotion that Owen did not understand welled in him. "You have been a good father," he choked. "Not always cheerful, but you provided a good home."

"But I did nothing to help you understand. I blocked you at every turn."

Owen started at a familiar, haunting sound outside. A wing flap?

Clearly his father heard it too. "You must hurry. Take the book and go. I will tell them you are in hiding. That you gave the book to the chosen one."

"Chosen one?"

"Hurry!" his father said.

Owen rushed into the next room and climbed the shelf to grab the Medusa bookend. He pulled and the case opened.

Owen's father touched his shoulder. "You are an old man's only hope," he said, his lips trembling. "I'm so sorry. It is my last wish that you might forgive me."

Owen shook his head. "There is nothing to forgive," he whispered.

"You may not want to return," Mr. Reeder said. "But I will keep this entrance open if you ever wish to."

The sounds outside grew louder. Flapping, crashing, banging.

"Thank you," Owen said. "I wish you peace. I will see you again."

"Yes, but you may wish you hadn't."

And with that, Owen was gone.

☩

The man grabbed the bookend, and the bookcase closed. He removed the Medusa head and smashed it on the floor.

The front door rattled, and he dragged himself toward it as if he had lead weights in his shoes.

In flew Karl, wild-eyed and pacing like a hungry dog.

"He is gone," Owen's father said. "You missed him."

Karl's eyes burned. "You let him go?"

"He was mad and spoke gibberish. Something about finding the Wormling. I sent him through the tunnel. The Slimesees will take care of him."

Karl grinned and clenched his fists, delight showing in his eyes. "The Dragon will be pleased."

36

Into the Abyss

Owen descended the stairs past
the familiar glow of the torches
along the wall. It was after midnight.
He was as quiet as he could be, hoping
not to alert the Slimesees. He laid his
backpack on the table and wrapped his
cherished *Book of the King* in a plastic
bag.

Owen had not been able to study
the book his father had given him, but
the title intrigued him: *Do-It-Yourself
Legacy: Remembering the Ancestors
You Never Had*. He pulled it out and
flipped through it as he walked, seeing families together around a dinner
table. Others were individual portraits.

Owen came to a page with an oval-shaped hole in the middle, and he paused near a flickering torch. Around the hole were pictures that featured women in pioneer costumes. Owen stopped when he saw a picture of his mother, hair down to her shoulders and wearing a modest, one-piece bathing suit. Her face bore the same serious look.

Owen pulled her picture from his backpack and removed it from the frame. It fit perfectly in the hole in the album.

When Owen heard water splashing at the other end of the tunnel, he stuffed the books in his backpack and took out a candy bar. He placed it on the table and scurried to the other side of the room. What better way to lure an animal than with a chocolate-and-peanut-butter-filled bar? While it was sniffing and then devouring at the table, Owen could slip into the tunnel and cross the water to the portal.

The book described the Slimesees as a sentry at the portals near the Highlands, whatever that meant, and that it was charged by *the evil one* with preventing anyone from crossing the water into the protected area of *the sandbar, where the worm is loosed and the journey begins.*

Owen wished there were some kind of an incantation that would cast a spell on the Slimesees, but the book was strangely silent about such things. He recalled a sentence from the book that said, *Nothing good is ever easy.*

✦

If you were a Slimesees, tongue slithering in and out, eyes accustomed to the darkness, able to exist in and out of water, you might have enjoyed the prospect of a teenager with food. After decades of feasting on decaying fish and putrid matter at the bottom of the watery crevasse, you might welcome a candy bar.

But to a Slimesees, the big catch was not the candy but the boy himself. Perched in the shadows of the ceiling, blending in with the rock and moss, the Slimesees bided his time until the boy moved into the tunnel. Here there would be no escape. And if the boy happened to fall into the water, even better. That always made the meal that much more satisfying. Death came quicker for humans in the water, which meant less thrashing about while being devoured.

A long, sticky, green string of drool ran down the being's jaw to the ground. The Slimesees crawled across the ceiling and to the tunnel entrance. The boy wasn't there. He had to be moving toward the water. Toward the portal.

Perfect.

✦

No sooner had Owen carried a torch into the tunnel than instinct told him something was behind him. He ripped off his shoes and socks and shoved them into his backpack. This would make him faster and provide more traction in the mud and slime. Maybe.

He reached the other end and edged close to the water. The sandbar had seemed only a few feet away before, but now the water looked a mile wide.

The surface of the water was still, which made Owen shiver. If the Slimesees was behind him, what had made noise in the water before?

Pitter-pat, pitter-pat echoed inside the tunnel. Then a growl and a sharp intake of air. Suddenly Owen's flame went out.

Owen was out of options. As the noise grew closer, he took a deep breath, pulled the straps of his backpack tighter, and plunged into the dark, icy water.

37

The Vortex

Owen had read that air in the lungs helps you float, so he took a breath and tried to fill them like an inflatable toy. But having never learned to swim made fear rise in him. He poked his head above the surface and panicked when it was clear the edge he had just leaped from was now miles behind him. And the sandbar near the portal—the one that had looked close enough to toss his backpack to—seemed an equal distance the other way. Now there was sky where the cave ceiling had been. And this was not just in his mind. Owen was bobbing in the middle of some enchanted waterway surrounded by the vastness of an ocean.

It expanded after I jumped. But why? And why didn't the book warn me?

A gentle wave propelled him toward land—toward the portal. So maybe he would make it. Maybe he wouldn't drown. But no sooner did this hope ascend within him than he turned at a ferocious splash behind him. The water stilled. The sky darkened. And the wind began to churn. The water beneath him circled like someone had pulled the plug in a bathtub.

Owen kicked against the cyclone vortex, but down he spun, sucked into the water hole. Just before his head was pulled beneath the surface, he spied a jagged, dark green fin several yards behind. It did not cut through the water straight and true like a shark but rather undulated, dipping and popping up, showing rippled skin.

Owen flailed, choking and sputtering and trying to rise, but the water engulfed him, and all he could hear was the throbbing of his own heart.

The Slimesees was a poor, ugly
creature fashioned by the Dragon
through years of crossbreeding and
manipulation. He had a single purpose:
to guard the portal and eat anything
that tried to get through.

One special ability the Slimesees
possessed was his capacity to sense fear.
He had created the cyclone beneath
the surface, and as Owen struggled
against it, the Slimesees picked up on
his panic and knew a good meal was
not far off.

He raised himself out of the water,
threw back his head, and let out a
bloodcurdling scream of anticipation
that also served to scare other animals

away from his prey—at least the ones that had survived. The Slimesees dived, shooting through the side wall of the cyclone and hovering there opposite the spinning Owen.

⧊

Owen feared drowning, was petrified of the Slimesees, and was even scared of how scared he was. As Owen's head rose out of the vortex, gasping and struggling to stay afloat, he wrestled with his backpack, air bubbles escaping as he unzipped it and reached inside for the plastic bag.

The Slimesees was staring, seemed to be calculating, preparing, waiting for just the right moment to spring and devour Owen. Through the thrashing water the boy noticed muscles tightening against green scales and the narrowing of those serpentine eyes. When the Slimesees sprang and shot like an arrow toward Owen, teeth bared, a feral missile intent upon tearing him limb from limb, Owen held *The Book of the King* out before him.

The Slimesees, stretched to full length, mouth open, looked horrified. His eyes widened, his tiny ears flew back, and he shrieked.

Owen recalled words from *The Book of the King* and spoke them boldly in a watery whisper: "'The King commands you.'"

The Slimesees stopped in midair, hung there for a second like a cartoon character, and sank into the abyss. Flailing,

he plunged to the bottom, the resounding splash creating a
reverse cyclone that shot high into the sky.

Owen was caught up in this current of water, wind, and
light and held the book as tightly as he could as he surged
upward with the force of a billion carnival rides. The cyclone
reversed from the inside out and blasted Owen into the air
like a cannonball.

Suddenly something rose before him, and Owen braced for
impact. But as if he were riding a flume, he slid down what was
left of the funnel and was deposited harmlessly in the sand.

The book was under his arm, his backpack still snug around
his shoulders. Owen threw sand in the air and scooped up
more, then danced around the tiny beach, laughing from the
belly. He had survived the Slimesees and the water and the
cyclone, all because of a few words from the book.

Mr. Page had spoken of the power of the book and its words,
but Owen had never dreamed of anything like this. He sat in
the sand and began to read, one eye on the water. The cave
ceiling had returned and it was dark again, but he was grateful
for a little light.

Mucker peeked out from between the pages and wiped his
head as if brushing sweat from his brow. Owen placed him in
the sand and watched the tiny creature inch along, making a
track to the stone wall. Owen followed and sat with his back
to the wall. A few palms made him feel sheltered, although he

worried the Slimesees might return or send a friend or brother for revenge.

Owen felt drawn to a section of the book titled "Making the Journey."

> Do not worry about what lies behind you, for yesterday is gone. Do not be concerned about tomorrow, for your path is prepared. Concern yourself with today and choose what is good. Work with a whole heart.

Mucker crawled up Owen's leg and onto his hand. Finally he moved to the edge of the book and turned back several pages with his head. Owen was fascinated that Mucker knew what he was doing, almost as if he had written these words.

Mucker crawled to the middle of a page, and Owen read:

> Prepare yourself for the journey with rest. Sleep and dream great dreams, for it will be difficult to get to the other side.

Owen yawned and stretched and rubbed his eyes. The ordeal in the water had left him exhilarated, but now every muscle and bone went limp. He used his backpack for a pillow, stretching out in the sand.

39

Deep Slumber

Owen dreamed he was back at
Tattered Treasures, his father
behind the counter, head down. Owen
felt a deep desire to hug him, but as
he moved toward the man, he realized that this was not his father at all
but someone he had never seen. The
face was gnarled and angular, a sharp
nose jutting, shaggy eyebrows dancing,
and piercing red eyes that seemed to
belong to some reptile rather than to
a man.

Owen ran upstairs, but the man followed, changing form as he ascended.
Owen closed and locked his bedroom
door, ran to the window, and opened
it, then changed his mind and dived

into the closet. He buried himself deep in the back, peeking out through the hanging clothes, watching as his bedroom door appeared to bubble. The glass knob melted. Then the door was consumed by fire and vanished.

His room burst into flames, shattered and blackened embers floating about. Some fell on his bed and ignited the blankets and pillow. A ghastly smell filled the room, not just of smoke and fire but acrid and bitter, like death itself.

Owen stood still, trying to breathe, when the man entered and surveyed the area. He sneered at Owen's book collection, then picked up something from Owen's desk.

When he spotted the open window, the man took a deep breath and his back began to change. His clothing ripped open, revealing cracked skin, scales. The transformation was hideous, but Owen could not turn his eyes away. A huge tail appeared with a V-shaped appendage at the end. Hands and arms grew scales and muscles rippled. The man's shiny head grew rigid scales, and a snout extended. Owen was certain the being would be able to easily sniff him out now.

When the beast turned, Owen saw the same terrible red eyes, now in the body of a great dragon. As the being grew, the room could not contain it, and with a snort and a thrust of its horned head, it forced its way out the window, tearing out much of that wall.

Owen hurried to his desk where the frame holding the picture of his mother lay cracked, the picture torn. His mother's head was gone, and rage filled him. The Dragon had stolen his only connection with his mother. He whirled to face a gigantic hole in the wall.

Red eyes stared back. And then the great mouth opened, and searing heat and flames shot at him.

40

Toward the Portal

Owen awoke in a sweat, hands full of sand. He found the book and cradled it to his chest. There was no sign of the Slimesees, only his own footprints—and Mucker's tiny trail.

Mucker!

Where could he be? Eaten by some bird or bat?

Owen turned at the sound of scratching and found Mucker munching his way through the round dragon portrait etched into the stone wall. How could a worm eat through rock? His speed was amazing. Mucker would pull back his lips, bare his sharp teeth, and tear away. He had eaten about half an inch of the dragon's body and already he seemed bigger, his body thicker and more round. How could that have happened so quickly?

Seeing Mucker eat made Owen hungry too. He dug food from his backpack and devoured it in a few bites. Then he sat back against the wall again to read. Mucker crawled up his arm and perched on his shoulder for a moment, then moved back to the wall.

> The power of words will be evident as your journey begins. To breach the portal you will need patience, a steady eye, and consistent reading, for with each word you will proceed closer to your goal. Once you begin, there is no turning back, for the Mucker can lead in only one direction. Keep reading, despite any fatigue.

Owen was not simply heading to another realm. Everything in his life had led to this moment. In one way, he had been trained for such a trip, and in another, his education was just beginning.

The next time Owen looked up from the book, he found a huge pile of gravel. Mucker's tail squirmed above him. The little thing had created a hole three feet wide.

By now nothing Mucker accomplished could surprise Owen. So he continued reading, totally engrossed. Parts of the book he could not understand, and he had to read slowly and often read the same paragraph several times. Some things, he knew, he would not understand until he was in the middle of doing them.

An hour later he became aware that the noise behind him had ceased, and he turned to see what Mucker was up to. Owen yelped when he faced an enormous head and teeth that could tear him to pieces. But it was only Mucker. A much, much bigger Mucker.

Owen stood, surrounded by gravel, to find the hole so deep he could not see its end. Owen strapped on his headlamp, grabbed his backpack and the book, and climbed atop the gravel to where he could squeeze through and follow Mucker.

A strange orange-green glow came from Mucker as he led the way. Owen scooted along, pulling the backpack. When they reached the end of where Mucker had dug, the creature stopped, as if waiting for Owen to read again. When Owen dug out the book, Mucker started in again, chomping and chewing, clearing dirt and rock from before them. Mucker chewed with his ever-growing teeth, then brushed the residue back with his body, pushing it around Owen.

Mucker was growing with each chomp of dirt, so he had to be swallowing some of it. It made no scientific sense, but it seemed the bigger Mucker grew and the more progress he made, the more air came from the very pores of his skin, supplying Owen with all he needed to breathe.

Seven hours into the trip, Owen's eyelids felt like they

weighed five pounds. Mucker had accelerated and moved huge amounts of dirt and rock with every chomp. Owen could now kneel in the tunnel without his head touching the ceiling. He stopped reading long enough to feel the smooth sides, which reminded him of the ones under the bookstore. He had to wonder if Mucker had created those. Then he remembered he was to read despite his fatigue.

> Silver and gold pass through your hands, but a good friend lasts forever and is to be treasured above any material thing.

Owen wished he had a friend to share this experience, but who would have believed it? He was glad he didn't have to face the police or the principal or Gordan and his crew, at least for a while. This whole journey felt like running away, but he knew he would eventually have to set things right with everyone, including his father.

> A brother is born to walk with you through difficult times, but there is a friend even closer and more faithful than a brother.

As Owen read, Mucker tore more dirt and sediment from the walls. Mucker now weighed enough that he could crush Owen simply by rolling the wrong way.

Owen reached the end of the chapter on directions and then reread it. He did not understand what a Watcher was, nor could he comprehend what he was to experience when he breached the portal.

Owen was now able to stand, the top of the tunnel well above his head. It felt good to be fully upright, and as his reading speed increased, so did Mucker's chewing. With swiftness and urgency, Mucker angled down and the tunnel became so steep that Owen sat and slid behind his friend, finding it difficult to keep the book steady. He found a map labeled with names and mountain ranges and forests, and his heart swelled.

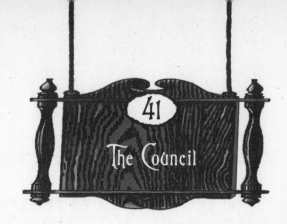

41

The Council

RHM rushed into the Dragon's war room at the top of the highest spire of the castle. From there the Dragon or any of the top warlords on his council could see the expanse of the kingdom. From the shards of glass that lay by the walls and the holes in the windows, it was clear that no one was safe from being thrown out.

RHM approached the thick wooden council table, surrounded by the Dragon and his underlings, and placed a piece of parchment before the creature. He stepped back. "Sire, there has been a report of a rumbling coming from portal number three."

"So soon?" the Dragon said. "What of the Slimesees in that region?"

RHM shook his head. "There was a disturbance—"

"Disturbance?" the Dragon snapped. "What sort of disturbance?"

"The water rose like a tsunami. We have not been able to track the Slimesees."

The Dragon closed his eyes and let the air expel from his lungs. Members of the war council moved back from the table, clearly fearing fire. The Dragon opened his eyes and glared at RHM. "How long?"

"Not long. The portal may have already been breached."

The Dragon slithered to the southern windows and peered through the mist. He scratched his scaly back. "So this boy must have found the Wormling, and the book is in his hands. But how much can he understand? How will he be able to go against us?"

Nervous laughter spread around the table. Dreadwart, the horned one, said, "But, sire, if we simply rid the kingdom of this Wormling and destroy the boy in the Highlands, we will not have to worry about any understanding, or in the worst case, uniting—"

"Silence!" the Dragon bellowed, eyes gleaming as he spun. "You were told never to use that word in my presence!"

Dreadwart turned, eyes clenched as if awaiting the fiery

blast. "Begging your indulgence, sire. I want only what is best for your kingdom. If we snuff him out now, we would not have to worry about his breaching the portal, let alone ultimately succeeding."

The Dragon turned back to the window, arms behind his back, head tilted. "If he has made it past the Slimesees, he will be most vulnerable when he reaches the Lowlands."

Dreadwart rose. "If you'll allow me, sire, I would be honored to root him out and complete the task the Slimesees failed to accomplish."

The Dragon turned, haughty. "Are you forgetting that he slipped through my talons as well?"

"Only in the Highlands, sire. And you killed the other. Your powers are diminished there, or you would have annihilated him."

"Silence," the Dragon said. "Your bleating tires me. Go then if you are so confident. And deliver his body to me." He turned to RHM. "Continue your search for the boy in hiding."

Dreadwart bowed and pressed his palms together in thanks, then strode from the room, his massive hooves striking the floor.

"And retrieve the book as well!" the Dragon called after him. "I do not want it falling into the hands of the rabble."

When Dreadwart was gone, the Dragon turned to the others. "Frankly, I am not sure Dreadwart can succeed. That isn't all bad. If this Wormling is the one and the book is the prophecy the King has long desired, perhaps we can use the lad for our own purposes. Seduce him. Make him a servant of the true master."

The council clapped and banged the table.

When the Dragon raised an eyebrow, they stopped and joined him at the window. Dreadwart crossed the bridge below them, his aides not far behind. The enormous beast's horns glistened in the mist, as did his sharpened hooves. On his back hung a black cape that reached the ground, steel spikes embedded into the fabric, decorated with the crest of the Dragon.

"If he kills the Wormling," the Dragon said, "our worries are over. But if the Wormling slips through and lives, we will use him. Either way we win. Eventually the kingdoms will be united under me, the true and sovereign king."

"Hail to the Dragon!" the others cried.

42

The Rumbling

Deep in the Valley of Shoam, as the morning mists began to rise above barren treetops and hills, the lonesome single note of a horn wafted its way down the hillside like a cool summer breeze. It was sustained with clarity and precision, and someone new to the land might have thought it simply accompaniment for another morning.

But no, it was a clarion call, signaling something new, something wonderful and terrible at the same time. A chance. A risk. A last-ditch effort to restore what the Dragon had long ago defiled.

Several homes, shacks with thin roofs and weathered walls, sat at the bottom of the ravine. Thin lines of smoke rose from chimneys.

A face appeared at the dirty window of the shack closest to the mountain. A fat hand wiped the glass, and tired and puffy bug eyes peered out. Scruffy beard. Red lips. Shaggy hair streaked with gray hung to the man's bulbous nose. He drew the hair back over his ears and listened. Then he withdrew from the window and threw on a cloak. He chose his barefoot steps carefully on the crude porch, avoiding rotting boards, then jammed on leather boots as worn and tired as the man himself.

He jumped past steps that looked like they couldn't hold his weight anyway, slid in mud, feet flying, righting himself to head up the mountain. But as he lifted his eyes to the hills, the single note blew again, and a look came over his face— hope, anticipation, eagerness—shining through a visage lined by years of hardship and worry.

For many years the man had lived under the threat of attack by the Dragon. That's why fear seeped through the skin and entered the souls of those in the Lowlands—too many years of wishing and hoping for the promise. The long-haired man ran through the trees, grabbing limbs, pulling himself up toward the sound. Needles released and limbs snapped. Rosin flowed and stuck to his hands, leaving them smelling of sweet pine.

Ahead of him small bushes shook, and through the sparse leaves and over the needle-matted ground raced a smaller being. Over the rocks and rills the furry face somersaulted and finally came to rest at the huge man's feet.

"Watcher," the man said, "why aren't you at your post?"

The Watcher stood four feet from toe to head. She bore the face of a terrier, with brown and blonde fur that shot back from her dark nose and tufts of hair over brown eyes. Dainty ears stood as upside-down Vs on her head, twitching with excitement as she brushed needles from her fur. Her mouth appeared more human than animal, and her lips still bore the imprint of the horn she carried. "Rumbling," she said, gasping. "Louder and louder. Inside the mountain. From the portal."

"It can't be a Wormling, can it?"

She nodded quickly, pointing. "The portal shook like an earthquake. You must come, Bardig."

They struggled up the hill while the rest of the village slept. Soon children would play in the rain-soaked streets, and animals would cry for their morning meals. Above the trees, shrouded in mist, yellow-backed birds with long legs, short beaks, and piercing eyes took flight, gliding then alighting on barren limbs near the rocks. One bird separated from the others and hovered over Bardig and Watcher as they climbed, pushing each other, pulling on branches, laboring to make it to the portal.

Bardig glanced at the bird and hurled a stone at it. It squawked and rose farther, high above the trees and the portal, flying toward the icy blue waters of Mountain Lake. The bird's wings touched the surface, disturbing the bird's perfect reflection for only an instant.

"I know I've sounded the alarm before," Watcher said. "And there were many other times when I thought I felt something and wanted to sound it. You don't know how many times."

"I can feel the vibrations from here," Bardig said. "You may have redeemed yourself this time."

"Really, Bardig?" she said. "A true Wormling? In my lifetime? On my watch?" Watcher used the horn as a cane to propel herself forward.

They passed the Marking Tree—the biggest in the forest—where Watcher carved a mark on the eve of each new year. She had circled the tree three times with marks, taking up where her father had stopped, and his marks ascended from the marks her grandfather had made. A female Watcher would have been unheard of in their day, but having seen no Wormling for generations, most now called them fairy tales. Watchers were laughed at. But a remnant few supported Watcher's family with food and supplies. After dark, of course. Always after dark.

And so the day her father had become too ill to climb the mountain and had confined himself to the small house

where her mother could bring him soup and bread, Watcher
had climbed to the mark of the Dragon and taken her place
on the smooth stone where, for generations, her people had
stood as sentries for the hope of the Lowlands.

"The very trees shake," Bardig said, panting, grabbing
a centuries-old stone wall for support. "So much moisture.
The lake will surely burst over the side and wash us away."

"Don't say that, Bardig. The water will never overflow its
banks."

"I'm talking about the shaking. It's—"

But the shaking stopped. They stood looking at each other
in the suddenly disquieting silence.

And then the earth above them burst open, and Bardig
had just enough time to pull Watcher behind the Marking
Tree. A shower of rocks and damp earth and moss and even
trees plunged toward them. They covered their heads.

Bardig peeked around the tree and yelled, "Mucker!"

Out of the great hole in the earth spilled the largest worm
he had ever seen. Dirty white, almost translucent, it cascaded
down the mountain, unable to stop. It finally reached the
Marking Tree, slamming it with the middle of its body, head
and tail plunging forward, wrapped around the tree like an
overgrown lasso.

Mucker was soft and spongy, and Bardig and Watcher stepped
onto its back and pushed themselves up. Watcher giggled as she

bounced, then slid to the ground. Bardig, slower and heavier, sank into the worm's soft underbelly, finally reaching the ground.

"Is it dead?" Watcher said.

Bardig walked above the animal, trying to find its head. "I've never seen one before, so I wouldn't know. Can you take the pulse of a Mucker?"

Another stream of dirt and rocks tumbled down the hill, and both covered their heads. A boy stood above them, dwarfed by the giant opening. In one hand he held some kind of pack, and in the other . . . what?

"The book," Bardig whispered.

43

Old and New Friends

Owen stood at the edge of the
hole, looking at a new world.
It was strange, but he would have to
study it later. For now, Mucker lay
motionless, wrapped around a tree,
studied by a hairy man with dark fea-
tures and an animal, mouth agape.
The man said something to the animal, and the two ran toward Owen.

Had they killed Mucker? Their
speed scared Owen, and he looked for
something with which to defend himself. He thrust out the book and yelled,
"'The King commands you.'"

The animal dropped to its knees in
the dirt.

The man followed, bowing before Owen. "Welcome, Wormling," he said in a deep voice.

"You know me?"

"We've been expecting you for many years."

Owen motioned them to rise.

The man towered over him, while the animal came up to his chest and looked at him with eyes as brown as the earth. The man introduced them and informed Owen that "Watcher alerted me."

"How did she know I was coming?" Owen said.

"The vibrations," Watcher said.

Owen fell back. *An animal that talks?*

"Do Watchers not speak in your world?" Bardig said.

Watcher frowned. "He's a human. From the Highlands."

"I'm not sure what a Watcher is," Owen said, looking more closely at the animal. "You aren't human, are you?"

"If I were human, I wouldn't be a Watcher, would I? I couldn't have sensed your coming or warn you about attacks from the invisibles. And—"

"Invisibles?" Owen said.

Watcher rolled her eyes.

Bardig sighed. "I can see you have a lot to learn. Let's start with your name."

Owen introduced himself and said he lived over a bookstore.

"You have more books than this one?" Bardig said.

"Hundreds. Thousands even."

"And you can read?"

Owen laughed. "Of course. Can't you?"

"It's not allowed. For anyone, human or otherwise."

"How sad. Well, we'll have to talk with someone about changing the rule. Now what about my friend?"

"Yes," Bardig said, "let's tend to the Mucker, and then I'll take you home. You must be hungry. How long were you in the tunnel?"

As they gingerly made their way down the steep incline to Mucker, Owen told Bardig he didn't know how long, but that he had begun after midnight in his world and that he had probably read the whole day. "After facing the Slimesees, I—"

"Oh, go on!" Watcher said. "You didn't battle the Slimesees!"

"I did," he said, describing it and what had happened. Watcher scowled.

Owen put a hand on Mucker's back. "Are you all right, friend?"

"I'm sorry to tell you," Bardig said, "that legend says a Mucker is good for one trip and that's all. Start out small, did he?"

Owen nodded.

Bardig shook his head. "They expand and move so much

earth and rock that their bodies just give out. And their teeth get worked to the bone."

Mucker's eyes were closed and his mouth slightly open. Indeed his teeth had been whittled to the gums.

"You did it," Owen said, fighting tears. "But I don't want to lose you. How will I get back without you?"

Owen heard sniffling and turned to see Watcher weeping. He feared he had gotten off on the wrong foot with her, but it seemed clear that she was having second thoughts about him. "What a faithful friend you are, Owen Reeder. If you have this much compassion for a lowly animal, how much more will you do for us?"

Owen stayed with Mucker, but the animal didn't stir. "We can't just leave him here," Owen said.

"The people will help us," Bardig said. "We'll give him a proper send-off."

44

Mustering for Attack

Portal three was near Mountain Lake, Dreadwart knew, and the village below was in the path of water that could wash the area clean.

How he hated the process of going from the kingdom of darkness and invisibility to the realm of light. Those in the Lowlands endured such squalor and earthiness and lived devoid of power and riches. But they had something even the Dragon did not possess. At least not yet. Such was the unspoken topic of each council meeting. The elephant in the room, as it were.

Dreadwart slipped through the clouds and became visible to the rabble below. He had little to fear.

The beings on land could not stand up to his weapons. All they had were sticks and stones and a few blends of metal. Nothing he couldn't defeat with one blow from a single nostril.

Dreadwart circled in the air until a minion returned to report the breach of the portal.

Dreadwart smiled. "The time has come, my faithful ones, to lay waste to this earthly imbroglio. We will leave not one stone upon another until we have rooted the vermin from the soil. Death comes from the Dragon and by my sword today."

"Dreadwart!" his minions cried.

Owen had slipped into the world of the Lowlands so early in the morning that Watcher's horn had roused no one and alerted only one man who was already up. But Owen could tell from Watcher's and Bardig's reactions that when the village discovered him, there would be fanfare.

The Book of the King indicated that in the Lowlands, a world not as sophisticated as his, wars would be waged. He could have no idea, of course, of his own role in the same, and he hoped he wouldn't have to think about it just yet. In truth, he was thinking more about his empty stomach and the loss of Mucker.

As the three made their way down the mountain, Bardig pointed out various houses and told of those who dwelt there.

"What's the smaller dwelling behind each house?" Owen said.

Watcher rolled her eyes.

"That's the scrumhouse," Bardig said. "You know, where you go to—to exercise your bodily functions."

"The scrumhouse is your toilet?" Owen said. "You have outdoor toilets?"

"I suppose you'd rather have yours indoors," Watcher said, shaking her head. Clearly she had gotten over her fascination with him.

Bardig's home proved cozy, with a warm fire and fruit sliced in a wooden basket on the table. The house was one big room combining the kitchen, bedroom, and living room. Four beams stretched from the ground to the ceiling.

Bardig motioned Owen to a chair. As soon as he sat, keeping his backpack snug on his back, a lump moved in the bed in the far corner.

Bardig touched the covers gently and bent, whispering.

A large woman with a jowly face and a white nightcap sat straight up, eyes wide. "A Wormling? In my house?" She squinted at Watcher, then at Owen, and tumbled out of bed, banging her knees on the floor. She struggled to her feet and made her way to Owen, sticking her face inches from his and studying him. "A real Wormling. And you've come to help?"

"He has a book in that bag," Bardig said.

The woman gasped, as if someone had brought all the gold in the world into her home. "*The* book?"

Watcher nodded, wiping fruit juice from around her mouth.

"Will you be staying long?" the woman said. "I suppose you have a schedule."

"I'm not sure," Owen said. "I've just arrived."

Bardig scowled at Watcher and took the fruit basket, handing it to Owen. "Take what you like. And I'll get you some flat meal."

While his wife studied Owen and frowned, Bardig fetched a wood tray draped with a cloth. He set it before Owen, removing the cloth to reveal what looked like smashed corn bread cut into small wedges.

Watcher reached around Owen, grabbed a piece, and devoured it, eliciting a wicked stare from Bardig.

"Thank you," Owen said. "It smells delicious." He picked up a piece, but it crumbled and dropped to the floor.

A small, catlike animal appeared from the shadows and scarfed down the crumbs.

"Good girl," Bardig said. He nudged the creature away with his foot when it began sniffing Owen's clothes.

Owen carefully put another piece of flat meal to his mouth, but before he could take a bite, Watcher grabbed his wrist, sending the food to the floor again. "Why'd you—?"

"Shh," Watcher said, ears twitching and the hair on her back standing straight.

Bardig and his wife looked terrified.

Watcher's pupils dilated suddenly, then closed to the size of a pin.

"What is it?" Owen whispered.

"An invisible—breaching the clouds."

"What does that mean?" Owen said.

Watcher scampered to the window.

Bardig pulled a huge sword from a cabinet near the door and handed it to Owen.

"Is that also a hatchet in there?" Owen said. "Let me have it."

"You are more skilled with that?"

"No. But the sword is too heavy."

46
The Day of Dreadwart

"Can you tell who it is, Watcher?" Bardig said.

Bardig, Watcher, and Owen crept out onto a path leading to the town center.

"I sense strength," Watcher whispered. "A battle-scarred being. Hoofbeats."

"A horse warrior?"

"Much stronger and larger."

"One of the council then," Bardig said. "That means they know the Wormling is here."

"Council?" Owen said.

"The Dragon's. But if you are who

we think you are—and obviously who the council thinks you are—why doesn't he come himself?"

"He already came for me. In my world."

Watcher smirked and shook her head. "If the Dragon came for you, you wouldn't be here."

"No, it happened. He chased three of us—me, a friend, and an old man. The man removed something from my foot so the Dragon couldn't find me."

"Old man?" Bardig said.

Owen described Mr. Page, and Bardig paled.

"It couldn't be," Watcher said.

"Couldn't be who?" Owen said.

Above them the air came alive with what sounded like helicopter blades.

Watcher pointed to the hillside. "Dreadwart. His hooves beat the sound of attack."

"Blow the alarm," Bardig said.

Watcher grabbed her horn and blew four strong blasts and a short one.

Within seconds people streamed from their homes and shacks along the path. Some exited scrumhouses, hastily zipping and buttoning. They searched the sky as the hoofbeats grew louder.

Owen was amazed at how many lived in so few homes. Most looked thin, almost skeletal, shawls draped around their shoulders against the cold. The Valley of Shoam was nothing like home.

"Dreadwart!" someone shouted, and the awful name was repeated dozens of times.

"Do not fear!" Bardig yelled. "This very morning Watcher discovered a Wormling! He will help fight the beast!"

"A Wormling?" many said.

Others chattered and whispered.

"Is that small thing a real Wormling?"

The crowds moved toward Owen, but when a fierce sonic-boom type blast shook the earth, they ducked and trained their eyes on the sky.

"If Dreadwart is an invisible," Owen said, "how did you know he was coming?"

Watcher sounded annoyed. "It's what I do. I sense the unseen."

"How am I supposed to fight—?"

"You'll see him," she snapped. "Or are you too scared to stand your ground?"

Bardig put an arm around him. "Don't worry, Wormling. Our world is not always this fearsome."

Dreadwart split the clouds and plunged to earth, a jet-black beast glistening in the rising sun, silver horns swinging like a bucking rodeo bull's. On his back lay a spike-studded cape, reaching to gleaming hooves sharpened to deadly points.

Dreadwart's tail was sheathed in metal and ended in a razor-sharp spear. Even a ring in his nose looked to be a weapon, and he swung it like a club. He opened his mouth to reveal long teeth like a tiger's. Anyone caught in his viselike jaws would be torn and crushed.

People ran toward their homes, but Dreadwart's tail snapped at a row of the claptrap buildings, and they exploded, wood and ceiling tiles flying, along with beams and logs and kitchen utensils and tables. The citizens of the Lowlands screamed and headed for the hills as the terrible day of Dreadwart unfolded.

The monster uprooted and toppled trees like toys with one kick. Children wailed and clung to their parents. Dreadwart moved toward a small red schoolhouse with crude swings hanging from trees. He lowered his head and drove his horns through the building, lifting it off its foundation. With a jerk of his head he threw the structure behind him, and it crashed against the hill.

Shooting a blast from his nostrils like a jet engine, Dreadwart dug his sharpened hooves into the ground and bellowed a ferocious roar. Even the birds fell silent as he scanned the village. "People of the valley," he said in a gravelly and foreboding voice, "the council has treated you fairly and allowed you to live in peace."

"When you allowed us to live at all," Watcher muttered.

Dreadwart's voice boomed across the hill and shook the trees. "But among you today stands a Wormling responsible for many deaths in the other world. He must be delivered to me to stand trial."

Bardig leaned close to Owen. "Is it true?"

"I didn't kill anyone!"

"If you harbor him," Dreadwart continued, "you will receive the justice he deserves. Your blood is on your own hands. Now send the Wormling forth!"

Whispers filled the woods as frightened villagers looked around. "Give him what he wants."

"If we don't, we'll all die."

"But the Wormling has done nothing to deserve this."

"Neither have we! Do you want to die for something he's accused of?"

Bardig raised a hand. "How do we know you will keep your word if we give you the Wormling?"

"What?" Watcher said. "You're not thinking of handing him over to—?"

Bardig squeezed Watcher's arm.

"I swear by the Dragon, you fool," Dreadwart thundered. Now softer, yet even more menacing: "I swear by your fallen King."

The people gasped and fell back. Could it be true?

A lone voice rang out like a tiny bell compared to the

power of the voice of Dreadwart. "Our King is not dead," a little girl said. "He lives!"

A murmur ran through the crowd as the child's parents muzzled her.

Dreadwart lifted his head. "Your King has left you and this realm. He was discovered in the other world." He paused. "And he was killed by the very Wormling who stands among you."

Owen felt the stares, including Watcher's. "He's lying," he whispered. "I never even met a king, let alone killed him."

Watcher skittered next to Bardig. "This is the one who's supposed to lead us to freedom? We should look for someone else in the cave."

"Present the Wormling now and there will be no further destruction!" Dreadwart said. "Otherwise, believe the fairy tales, and you shall all surely die!"

"Fairy tales?" Owen whispered.

"The prophecy," Watcher said. "The King's Son is to unite the two worlds and defeat the Dragon."

"How do you know the prophecy if you have no books?"

"The King told us before the castle was attacked and his children were taken. He told us to stay on guard and remain ever vigilant. He promised the Wormling would come, and the King's Son would be found. . . ."

"Give him up, Bardig!" someone shouted.

"Leave him to fend for himself!" another cried.

"If he killed our King, he should be punished!"

"If he is a true Wormling, can't he defeat this enemy?"

Bardig's voice carried to the monster and beyond. "Who among you can tell me one time when we've been told the truth by the Dragon or any of the council? Who among you believes our King is dead? Or that the Wormling killed him?"

"Who is this commoner?" Dreadwart growled.

"We are not many," Bardig said, "and we are weak. But we have truth on our side. And we have the book."

"The book?" Dreadwart stepped forward. "Give it to me!"

Hope surged through Owen. If Bardig could convince the others to stand their ground and face this enemy, they had a chance.

"Give him the book!" someone said.

"Yes, give it to him!"

"Will you spare the Wormling if he gives up the book?" another said.

"No! Deliver them both to me, and I guarantee the council will reward you. Land, property, livestock. And—"

Suddenly, Owen found his voice. The boy too afraid to speak at school decided that with lives on the line—including his own—he had to be heard. But he didn't choose his own words; he repeated some that he had read from *The Book of the King*. "'Live at peace with all as much as it is within you.

Give no one reason to slander your name or accuse you. But know that some will falsely accuse you and say all manner of evil things against you because you are related to the King.'"

The villagers stared at him, and while he felt exposed, almost as if standing naked before them, he somehow felt stronger.

"When the enemy comes," Owen said, "spouting lies and threatening, turn him back with these words, gaining momentum and volume. Say to him, 'The King commands you!'"

All eyes seemed to turn from Owen to Dreadwart, and on the faces of the Lowlanders came looks of expectation, hope, as if they believed that by simply repeating those words they could cause the terrible beast to burst into flames and disintegrate into dust that would blow away in the wind. Then they would dance, free and jubilant.

But no one spoke.

Dreadwart pawed the ground, snorting, then charged the villagers.

With Watcher pulling at his sleeve, Owen and the rest did the only thing brave people do when confronted by overwhelming evil and strength.

They ran.

47

The Return

They ran for trees that could not possibly protect them.

They ran past rocks and jumped streams where Dreadwart could not possibly miss them.

They ran thinking of nothing but survival, some carrying children, some hanging on to strips of clothing as their children pulled them.

Watcher grabbed Owen's sleeve, and the two hustled up the steep slope toward the newly dug cave. Did Watcher know some secret passage? Or did she have a plan to defeat this monster?

Owen turned to see the only one who had stood his ground, planting himself like a tree in Dreadwart's path. Owen whirled Watcher around to point out Bardig, standing there with the giant sword that looked like a toothpick in the face of the great snorting, charging demon bull. The beefy man deftly stepped aside as the bull ran past him and stopped.

"Prepare to die, Lowlander!" Dreadwart roared.

"Come, Watcher," Owen said, scrambling up the mountain. "He's buying us time."

Bardig wounded the bull, striking him across one eye. Dreadwart screamed and rubbed his face in the dirt. Bardig advanced on the beast again. It rose just as he reached it, and the tip of a horn pierced the man and sent him flying. With Bardig lying still and bleeding, Dreadwart turned to pursue Owen and Watcher, leaving a path of destruction on the hillside, mauling trees and people. But he did not slow to finish off any of them. Apparently only the Wormling was on his mind.

Some tried to roll stones down toward Dreadwart, and they bounced and picked up speed as they cascaded. But he sidestepped them like pebbles and seemed only to gain more resolve.

Owen pulled Watcher to the entrance of the tunnel.

"He knows where we are, Wormling," Watcher said, disdain in her voice. "This is a dead end."

Dreadwart bellowed, "I will kill you, Wormling! And I will breach the lake and send a flood upon the Lowlanders!"

"Leave me, Watcher!" Owen said. "Get as many to safety as you can!" When she hesitated, he pushed her out of the cave.

Owen turned to the book and began to read aloud. This was his strength, and it had brought him this far. If the last thing he did with his life was read the book until Dreadwart attacked, so be it.

> Fear does not live where love exists.
> Love always gives, always has hope, and believes the best.
> Love never fails.

Dreadwart reached the Marking Tree and, with a mighty heave of his tail, severed it in two, the top cracking and tumbling toward the village. "The day of the Wormling is over!" he howled, muscles tight, poised to leap toward Owen.

But something was different about the Marking Tree, other than the fact that it had been rent in two, and Owen couldn't figure out what it was.

Dreadwart sprang, his discolored tiger's teeth bared, his murderous tail swishing, and the spikes on his back aimed at Owen's heart.

Owen stood holding *The Book of the King*, fully expecting to be devoured, when Mucker sprang from behind a row of bushes and caught Dreadwart by the neck, chomping with what was left of his teeth and sending the beast to the ground. Dust flew and rocks rolled and the huge tail lashed, swinging and cutting. Owen had never seen such a terrible fight, and he knew the book had awakened Mucker, had prepared him for this moment.

When the squealing and the ruckus ceased, Owen made his way down the incline to where Dreadwart lay, bloody and headless. Mucker sat cut and battered but alive.

Owen fell on the worm's neck, overcome with emotion.

Owen found Watcher kneeling by Bardig, his wife cradling his head in her lap, weeping, gently brushing the hair from his face. Blood stained the man's shirt, and his legs lay at weird angles.

"You were the bravest of all," Owen managed. "You stood up to him, though your weapon was no match."

"Our weapons are the very words of your book," Bardig rasped. "May the weapons formed against you fail, Wormling. Be faithful in the smallest of things, and you shall see greater things than these." And he closed his eyes.

On a hill far away, under a fresh blanket of dirt and stone, they laid Bardig and others taken by Dreadwart's charge. Bardig's wife asked Owen to read from the book.

A brother is born to walk with you through difficult times, but there is a friend even closer and more faithful than a brother.

Late that day the sun set orange and red and purple on the Valley of Shoam.

Epilogue

Life, dear reader, is a mixture of sadness and joy and everything in between, but it is what you do with the "in between" that counts. Owen Reeder was beginning to learn this, but just beginning.

We have endeavored to tell you the whole story of his life thus far and will continue with Owen through even bloodier battles and more horrifying figures who seek his life. But for now, we must leave you with the image of Owen placing the book in a hidden spot and retracing his steps to the place the villagers had taken Dreadwart's body. Owen and the recovering Mucker packed the entrance to the cave with dirt and stone so the enemy would not be seen by the flying beings above.

Dreadwart's minions would report what had happened to the council, and its full force would be aimed at Owen. But until then the people of the Lowlands had surprise on their side. And the Wormling.

Owen looked to the hills and vowed, "The Son is out there, and I will find him."

Owen hoped he and Watcher could somehow become friends, but her demeanor was still cold. There was so much to discover. So much to do. And she could be such a help to him. But only time would tell.

Owen could not help but think about home, Tattered Treasures, his father, Constance, Gordan, and Mrs. Rothem. And what would Clara think of his absence?

It all seemed so far away and yet so close. . . .

Owen pulled the photo of his mother from his backpack and studied it.

Watcher came close and gasped. "I know her."

"What?"

"The woman in the picture. Perhaps it is just someone who looks like her, but the resemblance is—"

"Where does she live?" Owen said.

"Far from here. The journey is dangerous. But I would take you if you desire it."

A woman who looked like the mother he never knew? Owen would love to meet her. And with this new information, Owen knew he must make difficult choices in the coming days. "Perhaps while I search for the King's Son," he said.

ABOUT THE AUTHORS

Jerry B. Jenkins (jerryjenkins.com) is the writer of the Left Behind series. He owns the Jerry B. Jenkins Christian Writers Guild, an organization dedicated to mentoring aspiring authors. Former vice president for publishing for the Moody Bible Institute of Chicago, he also served many years as editor of *Moody* magazine and is now Moody's writer-at-large.

His writing has appeared in publications as varied as *Reader's Digest, Parade, Guideposts,* in-flight magazines, and dozens of other periodicals. Jenkins's biographies include books with Billy Graham, Hank Aaron, Bill Gaither, Luis Palau, Walter Payton, Orel Hershiser, and Nolan Ryan, among many others. His books appear regularly on the *New York Times, USA Today, Wall Street Journal,* and *Publishers Weekly* best-seller lists.

Jerry is also the writer of the nationally syndicated sports-story comic strip *Gil Thorp*, distributed to newspapers across the United States by Tribune Media Services.

Jerry and his wife, Dianna, live in Colorado and have three grown sons and four grandchildren.

✦✦✦

Chris Fabry is a writer and broadcaster who lives in Colorado. He has written more than 50 books, including collaboration on the Left Behind: The Kids and Red Rock Mysteries series.

You may have heard his voice on Focus on the Family, Moody Broadcasting, or Love Worth Finding. He has also written for *Adventures in Odyssey* and *Radio Theatre*.

Chris is a graduate of the W. Page Pitt School of Journalism at Marshall University in Huntington, West Virginia. He and his wife, Andrea, have nine children, two dogs, and a large car insurance bill.

RED ROCK MYSTERIES

BRYCE AND ASHLEY TIMBERLINE are normal 13-year-old twins, except for one thing—they discover action-packed mystery wherever they go. Wanting to get to the bottom of any mystery, these twins find themselves on a nonstop search for truth.

CP0140

The Future Is Clear

Check out the exciting Left Behind: The Kids series